MW01128071

THE
GEMINI
PROJECT

THE
GEMINI
PROJECT

VAUGHN A. CARNEY

Copyright © 2020 by Vaughn A. Carney.

ISBN: Softcover   978-1-6641-4133-9
               eBook   978-1-6641-4134-6

All rights reserved. No part of this book may be reproduced or transmitted in any form or by any means, electronic or mechanical, including photocopying, recording, or by any information storage and retrieval system, without permission in writing from the copyright owner.

This is a work of fiction. Names, characters, places and incidents either are the product of the author's imagination or are used fictitiously, and any resemblance to any actual persons, living or dead, events, or locales is entirely coincidental.

Any people depicted in stock imagery provided by Getty Images are models, and such images are being used for illustrative purposes only.
Certain stock imagery © Getty Images.

Print information available on the last page.

Rev. date: 11/09/2020

To order additional copies of this book, contact:
Xlibris
844-714-8691
www.Xlibris.com
Orders@Xlibris.com
822297

To Rebekah – who put all the pieces of my puzzle together. Love always.

To David &
Susan
Best wishes
Jac
08/04/2023

Please refer to the Afterword, which summarizes the
Royal Family of Saudi Arabia, the House of Saud.

SEPTEMBER 11, 2001

JEDDAH, SAUDI ARABIA

Prince Bindar bin Ahmed, an Oxford student visiting his mother's modest villa in Jeddah, had spent the previous day discreetly tipping off a few close friends that "something major" was about to happen in Manhattan, and that they should immediately leave the U.S.

The fact that Prince Bindar was an outcast and outlier with respect to the royal family stemmed solely from his low-birth circumstances: his father, Prince Ahmed, was one of the "Sudairi Seven" brothers, all of them the principal sons of King Saud, founder of the Kingdom. But his mother was a nameless, faceless black Sudanese slave owned by Prince Ahmed, making Bindar a bastard. She was given her freedom, a small villa and an annual allowance, with the tacit understanding that Bindar was debarred from, and would formally renounce, any claim to royal succession. He and his mother were sent to Jeddah, far beyond the inner circles of royal prerogative in Riyadh, where his aunt joined them. A quiet life with his mother and her sister was his fate until a chance meeting in Riyadh with his powerful grandmother when he was eight years of age.

But on the afternoon of September 11, 2001, he requested a late lunch in his private quarters, with orders not to be otherwise disturbed. Then he settled in to watch the coming horror on his wall of television screens.

SEPTEMBER 11, 2001

WASHINGTON, D.C.

In Washington, D.C. Robert Perkins sat in the study of his Georgetown mansion, transfixed before the television screen for the remainder of that day with myriad mixed emotions, predominantly shock and a grudging admiration at what he had just witnessed.

Twenty-four hours later, after the perpetrators were revealed to be mainly Saudi, he was thrilled. A warm wave of euphoria washed over him and his heart leapt with the joy of this discovery. His mind opened in only one direction. Already he was calculating, having found the silver lining that the day's events had presented him. It was the perfect opening, a fortuitous opportunity that he could never have imagined. He decided to let no one in on his scheming except on a need-to-know basis. This was to be a long-term proposition, a marathon rather than a sprint. It would require airtight planning, perfect execution and measuring every step out there in the darkness.

But the payoff, the end result, would completely change the course of history and make everyone involved, himself included, the wealthiest and most powerful men who ever lived.

His first telephone call was to a former colleague from his days at Langley. Perkins already knew exactly who he wanted in his inner circle. The next calls went to Dallas, Houston and New York City.

SEPTEMBER 11, 2001

Tangier, Morocco

Prince Mohammed bin Salman, sixteen years of age and the favorite son of Salman bin Abdulaziz, the future king, was visiting his father at his palatial villa in Tangier. Prince Mohammed, who had watched the horror of the attack on television, rushed to his father's private quarters to awaken him from his afternoon nap with the news. Later that evening, Salman received an urgent telephone call from his brother, King Fahd, who ordered him back to the Kingdom immediately.

The Saudi royal family knew exactly who was behind the attack: Antiroyalists who sought to punish the U.S. for its support of the royal family. The House of Saud, otherwise known as the royal family, was commonly disparaged as a nest of kleptocrats, hedonists, perverts and money-hustlers. But who was behind the anti-royalists, their sworn enemies, pulling the levers out there in the darkness?

None of this was lost on young Prince Mohammed bin Salman.

SEPTEMBER 27, 2017

RIYADH, SAUDI ARABIA

Crown Prince Mohammed bin Salman ("MBS" to the popular media), the 33-year-old favorite son of King Salman, had pulled off a masterpiece of manipulation. His 81-year-old father was long rumored to be increasingly senile, likely the onset of Alzheimer's. At the urging of his impetuous son, he was relieved to cede more and more of the powers enjoyed by the monarch.

Salman, one of the last two of the "Sudairi Seven" sons of King Saud, detested living in the Kingdom for its restrictions and religiosity. He privately believed that Islam should be left largely in the mosques, where it belonged. The customs and strictures on everyday life in the Kingdom made it insufferable for him. He acceded to the throne only because it was thrust upon him by tradition; to him, the crown was a chore and an imposition. Establishing a legal residence in Tangier, in a spacious villa, however, offered the best of both worlds: official residence in a Muslim city, with Spain's Costa del Sol only a fifteen-minute flight by private helicopter. It was there, in Marbella, where he had his most lavish villa, and where he moored his 350-foot yacht. This happy arrangement satisfied the tiresome optics of royal life in that he did not appear to be the sybarite he actually was. The thought of going back to the Kingdom to live out his days was repugnant to him, but it also made him much more receptive to handing over day-to-day responsibilities – and more – to his son.

For his first move, "MBS", had his father summon the then-Crown Prince Nayef, Mohammed's first cousin and heir-apparent. Without any preamble, Nayef was given an official-looking document to sign; it was a sworn and sealed renunciation of any and all rights to the throne in exchange for a sum to be determined. Mohammed, orchestrating the meeting, smilingly offered the sum of five billion Euros. Nayef, shocked and angered by this ambush, was now hotly offended by the proceedings, and said so. Mohammed, his smile gone, face tight and grim, made a second offer:

"Four billion Euros."

Nayef then understood that this was a power play, a deadly form of extortion, where Mohammed was holding all the cards. Nayef insisted on entering the amount in the document, then in resignation signed it in triplicate.

King Salman immediately named Mohammed as Crown Prince, and his accession to the throne was secured.

NOVEMBER 4, 2017

RIYADH, SAUDI ARABIA

On November 4, 2017, Crown Prince Mohammed bin Salman, "MBS", stunned the Middle East and the world by ordering the surprise mass arrests of over 200 prominent Saudi businessmen, including members of the royal family, on the flimsiest of pretexts: charges of public corruption and conflict of interest. It was an unprecedented act of ham-fisted ruthlessness, topped with a callow naivete.

An entire wing of the posh Ritz-Carlton Riyadh had been cordoned off by Saudi Internal Security, and the detainees were upon arrest immediately stripped of their cell phones and PDAs, along with their belts, shoelaces and wristwatches. Doors to the hotel rooms were to remain wide-open at all times. All televisions, radios and telephones were removed from the rooms, and newspapers were forbidden. Contact with all outsiders, including family and attorneys, was prohibited. Among the most prominent detainees were Prince Alwaleed bin Talal, the billionaire international businessman, and Prince Bandar bin Sultan, former Ambassador to the U.S.

All of those imprisoned found themselves exiting various stages of shock as the rules of their detention were explained to them. They were given a choice: Confess to the trumped-up lists of offenses and pay up, or refuse and face trial, certain conviction and imprisonment. Some of the detainees were blindfolded while being questioned. Others suffered health crises under the nonstop browbeating and crude extortion, and were refused medical care. There were unconfirmed reports of physical beatings. Two or three deaths were also reported, but not confirmed.

It was estimated that over 100 billion Euros were extorted from the victims of this primitive shakedown. And to add insult to injury, upon release, all of them were required to wear electronic ankle-bracelets so that their every movement could be monitored. Formal and express permission to leave the Kingdom was suddenly required. The detainees, while attempting to put the best face on the matter, were inwardly seething with rage.

Crown Prince Mohammed had foolishly antagonized some of the most powerful people in the world. The sheer indignity and public humiliation would never be forgiven, or forgotten. Even with the most extensive personal security in Saudi history, Crown Prince Mohammed bin Salman was deemed, in private, a dead- man walking.

—— ⁓⁓⁓◦◦◦◦⁓⁓⁓ ——

NOVEMBER 4, 2017

NEW YORK, N.Y.

Prince Bindar bin Ahmed sat having tea with his mother and aunt in their floor-through apartment just beneath the penthouse in Trump Tower, overlooking Fifth Avenue and Central Park. The upper floors were strictly private with extremely tight security, protected by armed guards, metal detectors and multiple cameras. Considering the number of Russian oligarchs who lived there, this level of security was not unusual. It was for this reason that Bindar chose to wait out the current crisis in the relative safety – and anonymity – of New York City.

Bindar, now fortyish, tall and handsome, cut an impressive figure in his Savile Row suits and accessories, and hand-lasted John Lobb shoes. He was conveniently out of the Kingdom and incommunicado when Crown Prince Mohammed imposed his draconian orders, as he had been tipped off by a high-level American contact. Many royal family members, fearing for their lives, were hiding out in London, living quietly in Mayfair and South Kensington. Others were hiding elsewhere overseas. Many of them feared for the lives of family in the Kingdom, and were effectively underground, terrified that one false step, one careless comment, could bring harm to their loved ones at home.

Always an outlier among the royals due to the circumstances of his birth, Bindar was never taken seriously. For the illegitimate son of Ahmed - the youngest of the "Sudairi Seven" brothers – life for this Prince did not stream with usual possibilities. His Sudanese slave mother meant that Bindar could have no meaningful seat of leadership. Of course he would be well cared for, being as how his father was a "tall prince" and full brother of King Fahd, but he would forever dwell on the fringes of the royal family. It was even more damning when his father, Ahmed himself, commonly viewed as a weak-minded pleasure-seeker, was removed entirely from the line of succession, meaning that neither Ahmed nor any of his legitimate sons could ever accede to the title he and all his brothers savored: Crown Prince. It was a bitter pill for Ahmed, but it infuriated his principal wife even more, because it meant that all of *her* sons were forever locked out from the inner sanctum of the royal family. And all because of that Sudanese whore.

Due to the circumstances and provenance of his birth, Bindar was largely ignored by the royal family. As a child, he was allowed to visit his father in private once or twice a year. It was during one of such visits, after Bindar had just turned eight, that he had a chance meeting with his grandmother – the formidable and powerful Hassa Al Sudairi, King Saud's widow. Almost immediately she recognized something compelling in this grandson, and demanded that he be brought to Riyadh to be properly educated and to live as a member of the royal family.

Hassa observed that Bindar, unlike most of her other grandsons - his wastrel, frivolous half-brothers and cousins - was serious, extremely bright and ferociously ambitious, and her heart went out to him because for all practical purposes he was an orphan. She airily dismissed her frivolous grandsons, once pithily commenting that "All they wish to do is eat American hamburgers and drive fast cars." Admittedly Bindar *was* a bastard. But he was her grandson by blood, which meant more to her than anything else. She took him under her wing, mentored him, and relentlessly pressured her seven sons to promote the boy within the royal family. He commenced his formal education with the other young royals, in Riyadh, and it was here that he began to make his mark with an extraordinary intellect and analytical ability. His academic accomplishments put him head and shoulders above his dullard cousins, and he was sent to the ancient and famous British boarding school, Harrow, in north London, where he continued to excel. He later earned first-class honors at Balliol College, Oxford, and a master's degree in international relations at Harvard. He returned to the Kingdom, joined the Saudi Air Force, and rose to the rank of Lieutenant Colonel as a fighter pilot – a highly unusual career path for a Saudi royal. But Bindar understood and accepted as an article of faith that in the desert, whoever controls the air, controls everything that happens on the ground.

Yet none of this seemed to mean very much among the royals of his generation and their elders. He was offered a position as an attaché at the

Saudi Mission to the United Nations, which he viewed as a palpable insult and a slap in the face. As far as he was concerned, his assigned role was no better than that of a glorified tea-boy. In the meantime, his dullard cousins were given the plum, do-nothing positions in government. So he decided to go into the aviation and arms business, where his military connections would help, and where there would be no limit on how much wealth he could amass. His sphere of influence in the Kingdom was the Saudi Ministry of Defense and Aviation, where he cultivated close and profitable relationships with U.S. military giants Boeing, Lockheed, Northrop Grumman, General Dynamics, Textron Bell Helicopter and Raytheon, to name a few. He represented all of them in sales to the Kingdom, and amassed a fortune – which he kept offshore and in strictest secrecy. Nobody in-Kingdom knew exactly how much he had stashed overseas.

Crown Prince Mohammed was vaguely aware of his older cousin, but dismissed him as irrelevant and no threat because of the lowness of his birth. Bindar knew that he was largely under the radar, but still visible. All he had were his mother and aunt; there were no other close relatives to be seized and held for ransom to drag him back to the Kingdom. At the moment, the three most important things to him were outside the Kingdom and beyond the reach of Prince Mohammed: his mother, his money and his secret family in London. Therefore, Mohammed had little leverage over him. And Bindar was determined to maintain this power dynamic at all costs.

Bindar, though unmarried, had been in a quiet, long-term relationship with a British barrister he had met at Oxford. She kept her chambers at Lincoln's Inn and practiced under her own name. They lived in a large, renovated regency townhouse in Belgrave Square, and had two school-aged children in one of London's most exclusive lower schools. The house was under constant security surveillance and protection.

NOVEMBER 7, 2018

WASHINGTON, D.C.

Robert Perkins kept several important men waiting in the conference room of his offices high above Georgetown. These were his cohorts, his inner circle.

His offices were held in the name of his own private limited liability company, Vanguard LLC, which also owned the entire building. His walls had been fully scrubbed for bugs and reinforced, and he had a steel walk-in safe in its own room. The whole building had been wired and alarmed, so that his security was impenetrable.

When he arrived, they smiled and greeted each other affably. They all could not help but notice that Perkins' killer eyes, the sharp intense eyes of a predatory bird, gleamed with delight. He did most of the talking.

"Well, gentlemen, let's get down to the business at hand. I take it the meeting in New York yesterday went well?" Without bothering to wait for an answer, he murmured, "Good, good. You know, Prince Mohammed has proven to be a real blessing in disguise. He has no idea how he's helping our own mission. It's perfect."

"How so, sir?" asked one of the men.

"Because he's creating the ideal distraction. The entire royal family is terrified of him, and walking on eggshells. That stunt he pulled at the Ritz-Carlton in Riyadh was a beaut, a real gem. He robbed the two-hundred most powerful Saudis with his crude shakedown. Oh, they'll genuflect, kiss his ring and say all the right things. But they want his head on a platter, and they have the power and influence to get to him. No amount of security can keep anyone safe when there's a price on his head. He can move, eat, sleep and crap surrounded by a small army of bodyguards, but it only takes one slip-up.

Anybody can be gotten to," he said, his voice dropping a full octave, and his eyes meeting everyone in the room. His meaning, and the clear threat, left no doubt about his resolve.

"Rob," asked one of the men, "we have it on sure authority that Prince Mohammed released his detainees only after having all of them fitted with electronic ankle-bracelets. They will now have to obtain his express permission to leave the Kingdom – for any reason. How can that help matters?"

"I'm glad you asked," replied Perkins. "Mortal fear, uncertainty and bitter resentment are the best sauces for what we intend to serve up. Prince Mohammed is unwittingly furthering our ends, setting the table, if I may torture the culinary metaphor."

"But what about his announcement of plans to take ARAMCO public?" asked the man. "Doesn't that complicate matters for us?"

"Not at all, not a bit. Another benefit for us, a huge advantage, really," said Perkins. "Say nothing about it now, let it crawl forward. Our mission will render that a non-issue. It won't matter if it does happen because they're only offering two percent of ARAMCO," he said confidently, fixing all of them with his blazing dark eyes. "We'll have the other 98 percent of it, and there'll be no problem squeezing out the minority shareholders."

Perkins let that last thought sink in.

"More immediate matters are on the table, though. We're due to make another payment to the Prince, this time in-Kingdom, in cash and diamonds, and off the books. Our contact has advised that we make this facilitation payment so that our operatives in-Kingdom are taken care of. We simply cannot move eighty-million Euros without detection, so we arranged to have it shipped in a diplomatic pouch, five million Euros in cash, seventy-five million in diamonds. It will be invisible to everyone except the Prince."

Perkins, a lifelong CIA senior operative, was a walking repository of above-top-secret information; he knew where all the bodies were buried, so to speak. The dirtiest and most sensitive jobs were his forte. He had come to believe that the most important chance meeting of his professional life was a curious one: a 1989 meeting with F.W. de Klerk, then-President of South Africa. They met at a classified Defense Intelligence conference at a private hotel in the London suburb of Windsor. Security was airtight. After a day's session, Perkins had gone to the nine-hole golf course adjacent to the hotel, and found President de Klerk at the driving range with his two personal bodyguards. Perkins introduced himself to de Klerk and suggested they play a few holes together. The conversation mesmerized Perkins. He found in de Klerk a highly perceptive and analytical man, the answer to the issue that most troubled him: How the coming white minority could continue to control the United States and other vital western countries. That clanging sound heard by Perkins was the scales falling from his eyes.

De Klerk asked Perkins to dinner with him that evening in the Presidential Suite of the hotel. It was during dinner that de Klerk explained his strategy for bringing a peaceful end to apartheid.

"You see, Robert, my most difficult problem has been getting the Afrikaners to go along. They fear universal suffrage because they know they will be outvoted every time, without exception. And yes, I have actively sold the idea to the ANC that voting will be the answer to all their problems, the panacea, if you will."

"But what about these demands for 'economic justice'?" asked Perkins.

"Our major focus now is *managing their expectations*. We contend that massive land reform and other such immediate wealth-redistribution measures would result in catastrophic losses – in flight capital, business shutdowns, and such. We say, let the marketplace be the rising tide that lifts all boats. I'll tell you, it's very convenient to have a disastrously failed black state right next door: Zimbabwe. They tried land and wealth redistribution and look at what happened there. Total political chaos, an economy and currency in free-fall. Mandela and the ANC are terrified of the same thing happening in South Africa. The black people of Zimbabwe are running away in droves, and where do they come? South Africa, a stable, prosperous country. We are not shy about reminding the ANC of this awful prospect, "dangling the gorilla", if you will. So in order to get the universal franchise, the ANC had to agree to kick the can of economic justice down the road for another day."

"What happens when that day comes?"

"It won't," replied de Klerk confidently. "The key here is to systematically co-opt the leaders of the ANC to do our bidding. They will all become instant millionaires and, in a few cases, billionaires. I needn't tell you what happens to a man when he suddenly becomes rich: he becomes much more conservative, because then he has plenty to lose. It's just human nature."

"I understand you had a hand in getting Zimbabwe cut off from the western capital markets and the International Monetary Fund," said Perkins wryly. "But I see why you had to do it. In the end, you own their leaders, and they serve as your buffer against the black majority."

"Precisely. And when the masses become restive, who do they turn on? Their compromised, corrupt leadership, of course. Who they will toss out of office and then empower yet another band of corrupt freebooters. We are the unseen hand in all of this."

"I understand," said Perkins.

"Your people in the States will face much the same crucible in about forty years, only it will be a lot easier for you because your people are not such a small minority. You know, I always admired your Mayor Richard Daley of Chicago."

"Mayor Daley? Why him?" asked Perkins, puzzled.

"Because he was a peasant who was cunning enough to rule as a master politician. He famously said 'It doesn't matter who votes. The only thing that matters is who *counts* the votes.' That was exactly how John F. Kennedy became president. That election was bought and paid for on the South Side of Chicago. And democracy was *built* to be compromised by money. That's why we see it as no threat at all. Not at all. Because we'll have all the money we need – and then some."

SEPTEMBER 24, 2019

RIYADH, SAUDI ARABIA

Trevor Osborne sat quietly and alone in La Trattoria, the best Italian restaurant in Riyadh, slowly and deliberately finishing his *osso bucco*, the signature dish of the place, pacing himself so that he would not finish that day's print edition of *The International Herald Tribune* first. He found himself idly recalling a popular adage among expatriate workers there: "When you come to Saudi to work, you bring two buckets; one for money, the other for shit. When either bucket is full, you leave." Because the sole and exclusive draw of the place is and always has been the mountains of tax-free cash. It had been almost twenty years since the 9/11 attacks in the U.S., and the ensuing furor had dissipated in the interim. The Bush administration had gotten the U.S. bogged down in Iraq, and there seemed no end to this folly, even under Obama.

And then there was the headstrong and dangerous Crown Prince Mohammed bin Salman, whose style tended toward ham-fisted and ill-advised muscle. There was no subtlety about him, and the entire royal family was tiptoeing around him for fear of attracting unwanted attention. Expats had no real concerns about what was largely a family squabble; as long as they stayed well on the side of the Saudi law, they were practically invisible to the natives.

The main dining room that evening was crowded and busy, with men only, as public restaurants did not permit women or children unless there was a "family section" – an area typically situated behind ornate screens that served women and children in such a way that the male diners did not have to be affronted by the sight of unrelated women in public.

Of course, he could have read just about anything he wanted online through his cellphone, but it was somehow more comforting to read a newspaper the old-fashioned way. It had become the high point of his day, a notion that many would have considered pathetic, but any westerner who has ever lived and worked in "The Kingdom" knows better. For he had quickly learned that Saudi is the strictest and most conservative of the Islamic states, the "cradle of Islam" and home to its two holiest cities, Mecca and Medina. Distilled down to its essence, the country is simply about oil, petrochemicals, sand and Islam. Slavery was not abolished until 1963. It is also a brutal, repressive police state masquerading as a theocracy, a successful ISIS on steroids. There is little public entertainment of any kind – no movies, music, theatre, nightclubs, cafes, bars, museums or other common western outlets. Prince Mohammed, as a showpiece for his "reforms", re-opened the cineplexes, but only to G-rated movies, and brought in World Wrestling Federation shows. Upper-class Saudi women were granted the right to drive, but many of them are still fearful because of continued harassment by the religious police – who delight in beating unveiled women and otherwise publicly humiliating women of *all* nationalities. Possession of alcohol brings a public flogging of fifty lashes and thirty days in jail. Saudi jails, known for their filth and brutality, make Rikers Island look like Fantasy Island; the outside life expectancy of any inmate is five years. Public executions by beheading – along with whippings, amputations, stonings and crucifixions – are featured weekly in Deera Square, nicknamed "Chop Chop Square" by the expats and guest workers. The punishments are then spooled repeatedly on local television so that no one could possibly miss the message. So how do the people engage in social interaction? They flock to the open-air souks down in the Old Quarter, or to the huge, ultra-modern, air-conditioned indoor shopping malls, where they wander aimlessly or shop with a vengeance. With the advent of satellite dishes, which the government had tried to ban, a window had been opened to western cultural influences, but up until then Saudi television consisted of just two channels: BBC News and The Disney Channel (which endlessly spooled and replayed the same animated features). But with the youth, it is all but impossible to block out western culture; close and lock all the windows, and it seeps in under the door. Trevor thought nothing of Saudi youth running around in Yankee baseball caps, Nike clothing and Air Jordans. One of the lifers told Trevor that ten years ago, that would have been unthinkable.

Tourism is not allowed, but foreign workers at all levels continue to flock there for the money. Many a retirement nest-egg has been handsomely replenished, many a small fortune has been made, and many a bottomed-out career has been turned around. Trevor was in this last category.

After paying the check and stepping out into the cool darkness of the evening, he decided to walk back to his studio apartment on the residential upper-floors of the enormous Al Khozama Hotel, a western-styled mega-hotel with its own shops, restaurants, spa, meeting rooms and amenities.

———————

He had been in Saudi now for nearly two years, serving as the American legal counsel for a Saudi firm, but really living in self-imposed exile. A major career setback and a ruinously expensive divorce back in New York had left him with literally nothing but his clothing and personal effects, so he seized upon this opportunity to change the channel, so to speak.

His law firm, where he had been a mid-level associate, suffered severe financial reversals after the loss of a major client and was forced to merge with another firm. And this merger pointedly did not include any of the "non-productive partners" and "non-essential associates" – meaning that anyone without a significant book of business was left behind.

Trevor intuited that he wouldn't even get that far, but for different reasons. Working late one evening at the office, he had missed dinner, so he took the fire stairs down one flight to the all-night cafeteria. As he entered the stairwell, he heard a muffled, angry female voice and the sound of a struggle. Down on the landing, an arrogant young male partner had pressed a female summer clerk against the wall, covering her mouth with one hand, and forcing his free hand up her dress to grab the elastic of her panties and tear them off her. All Trevor could do was stare at them in shock, rooted to the floor. The door behind him clicked shut, and they looked up to see him. The young woman took this opportunity to break away from him, slap him hard in the face and shout "You sick motherfucker!" before escaping. The young partner just looked sheepishly at Trevor, smiling and shrugging his shoulders.

"Let's just keep this between us, okay?" he ordered.

Trevor said nothing

When the woman immediately quit and sued the firm for $10 million, Trevor was subpoenaed as the sole eyewitness to give a deposition. Despite both implied benefits and veiled threats at the firm, he testified truthfully under oath, and when the presiding partner saw his testimony, the firm settled with her for $3.3 million. When Trevor shamefacedly told his best buddy from law school, Miles Braxton, what had happened, Miles chided him: "Now wait a minute, man. You fall on your sword to make this bitch a millionaire, and she didn't break you off some? Nothing? Shee-it, I woulda cut a deal with her upfront. No deal, no testimony. I'd have gotten a confession of judgment in the name of one of my people as the bagman. That way your fingerprints aren't on it. Next time some shit like this happens to you, call me first. Don't be a goddamned fool twice."

He was jobless, his marriage was cratered, the money problems intensified and, in addition to filing for divorce, his soon-to-be ex-wife was suing for alimony. It was time to disappear, "get in the wind", as a favorite uncle down in Jamaica loved saying. So he left behind a raft of grasping creditors, a rapacious ex-wife, and all of his illusions.

Several years of working here should, he surmised, right his financial ship and allow him to plot a suitable return to the states or, possibly, a relocation to Europe or the Caribbean, maybe placid Negril Beach, in Jamaica, whence his parents had emigrated to the U.S.

The thought of remaining in Saudi one minute longer than he had to was repulsive. Still and all, the sojourn there had allowed him to quietly think about his life, to assess, to plan – far beyond the tentacles of his tormentors. He had managed to save an impressive amount of money in those two short years, mainly because the money was tax-free, and because there was nothing to spend it on.

Leaving New York was as painful as he imagined it would be. Yes, he'd missed the brass ring, and yes, his wife had jumped ship in the immediate aftermath, marking him, in that high-stakes game, as just another two-time loser in a designer suit with a five-dollar shoeshine. She had found herself a hedge fund manager who was ostensibly on his way up, and Trevor had neither reason nor desire to continue contact with her. It was an old story. For his friends and acquaintances in New York, Saudi may as well have been Pluto; he'd tried to maintain his tenuous connections to them through e-mail and Facebook, but the caravansary of "making it" in Manhattan had moved on without him.

After the first few months in Saudi he heard from no one back in New York save his best buddy from Harvard Law School, Miles Braxton. Perhaps the others did not want their fetal ambitions contaminated by him. He was left to ponder the true essence of that harsh, acquisitive world – the tendency of so many people to simply vanish like a wisp of smoke, to become so thoroughly invisible that they might never have existed at all. When reality is this painful, he thought, escapism is not self-deluding; it is self-preserving, even healing.

But Miles was an interesting link to another dimension of discourse and trade. It was an unlikely friendship. They'd met as 1Ls in the registration line at Harvard Law, and Miles, a native Chicagoan, born and raised on the South Side, seemed to know all the secrets of everywhere he ever went, worldly-wise and street smart as he was. He had opened for Trevor the low door in the garden wall, a secret passageway to another universe of discourse. Trevor was a hopeless naif, a babe-in-the-woods by comparison.

Miles Braxton proved himself to be an enterprising fellow from the very beginning, totally in the tradition of Chicago hustlers. In kindergarten, he commenced his career of grifting and corruption by stealing from a senile grandmother's purse, purchasing large packs of cookies, then selling them to his much less astute little schoolmates in the Chicago Public Schools: two cents apiece or two-for-a-nickel. It was a huge hit.

A revelatory light came on and a career was born.

But Miles came by his gifts honestly; his father, Herman, had been a popular Chicago entrepreneur who Miles studied from afar and emulated in his dealings with a hostile world.

Observing his father, Miles discovered that all it took was will and nerve and cunning, his stock-in-trade.

In junior high, he talked his way into a job as a stockboy in a local auto parts business on the South Side, then began systematically stealing expensive auto components and selling them at discount to a rival business over on the West Side. There was literally nothing that Miles could not monetize to his personal advantage.

At fifteen, Miles, an indifferent and undistinguished high school student, saw a news feature on television regarding a minority uplift program called "A Better Chance", or ABC. The idea was to pluck promising minority students from rough public schools, and send them to New England boarding schools, thence to prestige colleges and universities. Miles stole transcript forms from his high school guidance office, forged a letter-perfect record of straight A's, forged letters of recommendation on the school letterhead, then paid an honor student to take his SSAT exam for him.

An aspiring football player, he was awarded a scholarship to the ancient and famous boarding school, St. Mark's, in Massachusetts, under the ABC program. It was here that he cultivated his polished, pseudo-waspy, J.Press persona, the Sidney Poitier effigy. It worked so well that he went all-in on it: a currency that inspired trust, one in which he both invested and traded. A confidence man and hustler, of course, had to inspire confidence. It afforded him valuable access – and the perfect cover for burglarizing the dorm rooms of wealthy prep school mates when they left on weekends. He took only expensive portable items – Leica cameras, Rolex watches, jewelry – things that would be easy to fence in the Roxbury and South End areas of Boston. He paid other students to write his papers, managed to steal or cheat on most exams, and hired a Harvard freshman to take his SATs. His performance at the school was solid but oddly uneven, yet his inflated SAT scores sealed a football scholarship to Colgate, where he blew out a knee in the third week of practice.

Miles felt that life wasn't exactly worth living after that, and actually considered quitting and going elsewhere, until a chance meeting with upperclassman Ethan Rothstein – a wiseguy from New York City who ran the sports gambling rackets at the school. Ethan had connections to all the mob bookies in Syracuse and Utica, and fronted for them in exchange for his vig on every wager. He also ran most of the high-stakes poker and crap games on and off-campus. But he saw something in Miles that appealed to his sense of mentorship, and so he apprenticed a willing student into his very lucrative hustle. Ethan would bequeath his hustle to Miles after he graduated and went on to become a highly successful professional sports gambler in Vegas. Not only did Miles retain this line of work, but he expanded into the Registrar's Office. He saw an ad for a student assistant, so he quickly applied and landed the position. The prospects were phenomenal. In exchange for cash, he secretly went into the transcript files and changed grades so that his customers, mainly fraternity thugs, could get into medical or law school, or simply just graduate from college. Miles told Trevor that the scheme was perfect and totally foolproof because both parties had a compelling interest in keeping it quiet, and were bound to a silence that would be guaranteed on both sides of the deal. Of course he changed his own grades and paid a professional test-taker to take his LSAT. When he got to Harvard Law, Miles had wangled a similar position in *that* Registrar's Office, where again, for cash, he would change grades so that these customers could work on Wall Street, or land clerkships and post-grad fellowships. For these services he charged much more – and got it. He also would regularly "work the secretaries", many of them young and single, charming them into giving him law exams in advance. This, too, could be provided for a fee. Miles was making law school work for him, and was using it to make a great deal of money. Trevor was convinced that Miles, slick as an okra, could turn just about anything to his personal benefit.

It was a lucrative business, as was the Great Alaska Gambit. Miles had assured Trevor, the timid and squeamish squire, the look-before-you-leap protégé, that each would easily clear $50,000 during the summer after the 1L year. They used a car delivery business to drive a new car to Anchorage, where they bought a jalopy and got jobs as SkyCaps at the airport. Trevor wondered how this vocation would lead to big money, and he quickly saw Miles's game. The Native-Alaskans (formerly called Eskimos) received monthly subsistence checks from the state and federal governments. Many of them were ignorant about money and what they could do with it, so Miles showed them: they would bring him their checks, which would be endorsed over to him; then he would randomly select a matched set of expensive luggage from a cart, and give it to them. It was like buying a box of surprises, and they loved it. Word quickly spread, and soon there was a stream of regular customers coming to them and purchasing stolen luggage with government subsistence checks. Trevor was initially uneasy about it, but Miles assured him that these losses were insured; all they were doing was sticking it to the insurance industry, who deserved to be fucked. They each cleared nearly $90,000 tax-free that summer, and flew back to Boston in first class.

For all this, Trevor was mildly distressed that he should be so easily suborned into a life of crime, for that was what it was. It was a barely perceptible stone in his shoe.

Trevor got another kind of education that summer. Miles taught him that America is not at all a secular nation; its true religion is ownership, with money as its God. In American culture, the confidence game or "hustle" looms as one of its major themes, along with self-invention and going on the lam, all of which are related in the swift-running undercurrents. Miles surely knew that it takes much more than cupidity and lack of scruples to make a master confidence man and hustler. The best of them possess a combination of keen intelligence, broad general knowledge, acting ability, resourcefulness, physical vigor, and improvisational skills which, otherwise channeled, would have propelled them to the top of any tricky trade or profession. Yet at the same time, most of his financial scams employed the mark's greed or corruption as a lever. In essence, he was merely hoisting the victim by his own petard, combining formal elegance with a careful imitation of legitimate business enterprise and rough-cut justice into what can only be called retribution. Once the victim's appetite was whetted, the game was as good as over, for greed has no patience. Miles's apparent sensitivity to the psychological needs of his mark, more than anything else, shed light on his ability to deceive and defraud. While in law school, he would run ads in newspapers from Seattle to San Diego, Boston to Miami, all major ports of entry for immigrants, promising expedited, low-interest business loans. The ads were outlandish puffery, promising the most unlikely terms. The victim would respond to the ad, and in return, receive lots of official-looking bank documents for completion. Then the victim would receive a telegram indicating that the loan was approved, pending final processing; a "service charge", usually a percentage of the loan or $10,000, whichever was greater, as a condition of closing the loan. At this point the victim would be salivating, could almost taste the money. He'd send in the fee and that would be it. There was, of course, no lender on the other end. And what made this such a lucrative scam is this: immigrants, especially the undocumented, have no recourse because they're afraid to go to law enforcement. Then, too, most people are ashamed to come forward and admit they've been so foolish. As Miles confided to Trevor, "It's harder to convince people that they've been swindled than it is to run the game on them."

───────

After law school, Trevor went straight to BigLaw, at the venerable old Wall Street firm of Milbank Tweed; Miles spurned a legal career and went to Kroll Associates, the world's most renowned security and intelligence firm. What Miles learned and practiced during the day at Kroll was exceedingly helpful in his sideline and avocation: his own private consulting firm for "sensitive matters". Miles could turn just about anything into his own personal hustle. This was why Trevor admired him - for his worldly-wise veneer, street savvy, his sheer will, nerve and creativity. He was a valuable friend to have, Trevor's "ace-boon-coon", in the street vernacular.

───────

The big Mercedes-Benz and Maybach sedans rushed silently by on Al Olaya Boulevard in the heavy evening traffic, and this had always amused and perplexed him. In a place where practically nothing was treated with urgency, what the hell was the rush? He observed the *mutawwa,* the religious police in their brown Volvos, slowly cruising near the curb, keeping a sharp eye out for infidels or unescorted women who could be harassed and occasionally beaten with rattan canes. Indeed, many stores and shops displayed signs in both Arabic and English: "Unveiled women not allowed." He merged into the evening shadows and moved briskly along, feeling as invisible as he actually was.

Trevor was ignorant of such customs when he'd arrived, and initially thought nothing of walking around during daytime prayers. He was soon disabused by the religious police, who, mistaking him for a Saudi infidel in western clothes, would roar up to him, jump out, and begin raging at him for not being in a mosque. Through pidgin English and primitive gesticulations, he was able to convey that he was a black American, at which point they would sneer before driving away. This was why he had taken to carrying his Igama – his work permit – everywhere he went. His employer, the law firm, held his passport for security, such that he could not leave the Kingdom without their permission. Occasionally he would wear the white thobe sheath favored by Saudi men, along with the red-checkered keffiyeh headdress for men, and it was as though he'd become invisible to them. He appeared to be just another local Saudi.

When he arrived back at the Al Khozama Hotel, he noticed in the wide, curved driveway a fleet of shiny, black SUVs, mainly Range Rovers with a few Escalades sprinkled into the mix. Typically such automobiles featured diplomatic plates and other indicia of official activity. But not these cars, which all bore nondescript Saudi plates. Something important was taking place here, but it was strictly private – whatever it was.

His residential-floor concierge, Manny, a pleasant little Filipino in hotel livery, saw him as he entered the huge lobby and eagerly approached.

"Do you need anything, Mr. Osborne?" he asked, smiling obsequiously and bowing his head.

"No, thanks, Manny," he replied.

"Well, you just let me know if you do, sir," he said, nodding. "I am at your service. If I'm not at my station upstairs, you can have me paged. And whenever you would like to play tennis again, let me know. I do enjoy it, sir, and I thank you for teaching me to play better."

"Thanks. I will," said Trevor.

Trevor had taken to playing tennis on the hotel's rooftop courts, usually in the evenings after the heat of the day had broken. With a shortage of hitting partners, he'd asked Manny to hit with him during the latter's evening break, and while he was just a beginner, Manny was a quick study and usually managed to get the ball back over the net. A distant but cordial friendship had developed, and Manny was clever enough not to presume upon it. Trevor knew that Manny and his younger brother, Ferdie, had both been recruited to work in the Kingdom, and that they lived among *les miserables*: the lowly, expat service workers who resided in squalor down in the Old Quarter of the city. They were typically Filipino, African, Indonesian, Pakistani and Lebanese, along with the Korean construction workers, all living in crowded, seedy rooming houses. Curiously, the Koreans seemed to be the only guest workers who enjoyed the public whippings, stonings and beheadings at Deera Square. They packed picnic lunches and treated these occasions as entertainment. Most westerners and Saudis were too squeamish to even witness such barbarity on television.

The Americans who worked in-Kingdom with ARAMCO and other oil industry servicers live well outside the cities, situated inside high-walled, self-contained compounds, little slices of suburbia with their own supermarkets and other amenities, set down in middle of the desert. They actually had their own Little League that regularly sent its all-star team to Williamsport. Saudis were strictly forbidden to enter these enclaves for fear of their being exposed to depraved western ways.

Trevor stopped at the front desk to pick up his personal mail and FEDEX packages, bought a *Vanity Fair* magazine at the newsstand, and headed for the elevator banks. It would be the usual tonight: cable news followed by some sanitized American movie, or reading until he dropped off to sleep. It was an isolated, lonely, antiseptic existence, but one which would allow him to reclaim such leftover life as he might have ahead of him. Having a girlfriend was completely out of the question; there were no unattached western women here, and Saudi women were strictly off-limits.

A group of sober-looking, dark-suited men, possibly European or American or both, argued in heated, angry tones, with voices rising as he approached the elevator bank and the open door. He boarded in a tense silence as the door closed. One man muttered to another "You fucking idiot" when suddenly and without warning, a scuffle broke out in the elevator, with two of the men wrestling and cursing in the cramped space and the others rushing to break it up. Trevor pressed himself in a corner as the two angry combatants were separated by the other men, still cursing and sputtering their rage. Trevor may as well have been a potted plant. They took no notice of him. The men, separated and temporarily pacified, trooped off the elevator on the exclusive penthouse floor, still cursing each other. But standing at the open door were two armed security guards whom Trevor had never seen before. He stayed in the car and pushed the button for his floor.

As the car headed down, he turned and saw that a briefcase had been left in the back corner. Reflexively he picked it up and took it with him, intending to hand it over at the front desk. Yet something – he could not imagine what – impelled him to take it to his room and open it first.

Shock and disbelief made him gasp sharply when he saw the contents, and for a moment he was paralyzed by the thunderous pounding of his heart and the roaring, surfy din in his ears. In a single instant, the world as Trevor knew it dropped away from him, leaving him alone on a cold and distant planet, where there was no gravity and nothing made sense anymore.

He suddenly understood exactly how a single rash, impulsive decision could become a whole, irreversible life.

SEPTEMBER 24, 2019

OVER THE RED SEA

"Good evening, ladies and gentlemen, this is your captain. British Airways flight 1331, nonstop service from London Heathrow to Riyadh, will be commencing its descent into Riyadh shortly. We will be entering Saudi airspace in about twenty minutes, so I would ask that you finish any alcoholic beverages or have your flight attendant remove them. All alcohol must be locked in the liquor cabinet before we may land. If you are carrying alcohol with you, please notify your flight attendant at once, as simple possession is an offense punishable by public whipping and imprisonment. Thank you for your cooperation."

Souheir Fahad, sitting in business class, finished her gin-and-tonic. She had requested tickets on British Airways because Saudia, the flag carrier of Saudi Arabia, did not serve alcohol at all.

She was stunning just wearing her designer jeans, expensive boots and a cashmere sweater, her long, black hair swept up, revealing a beautiful, heart-shaped face framing blazing dark eyes. But she knew the drill. All the Saudi women on the flight would grab their carry-ons and troop en masse to the lavatories to change from their stylish, expensive western clothes into their abayas – the ugly, shapeless, veiled black sacks that Souheir hated. She decided to wait until after the rush to the lavatories to don hers. It was a garment that she hated, and only wore if absolutely required. Because it marked her as a third-class citizen with almost no rights enforceable by law, a serf and a servant always subject to the whims of her male relatives.

While completing her two-year term of teacher training at NYU, she had found that her real passion was film. The West Village of New York was a magical, wonderful place, where she was totally free, happy and fulfilled for the six years she was in school there. She found herself auditing courses at the famous Tisch School of the Arts at NYU, going to indie film festivals, writing critical pieces for various journals, and dreaming that she might one day produce quality films.

Instead of what? Going back home to an oppressive, empty place for her, working in some all-girls school, teaching young women as hopeful as she once was, knowing that only frustration and suppressed rage awaited them, too. She had feared returning, feeling that she might never get out of that hellhole again. Yet this was a desperate mission to get her family's blessing – along with their continuing generous financial support - for her return to the US and film school in New York. She was hoping that they might see things her way, and she had already extracted a promise from her father, a prominent attorney, that she would not be forced into an arranged marriage, her worst nightmare, a condition which would eliminate any possibility of leaving. Souheir had no interest in marrying anyone at this stage of her life, but if it could only be a "love match", she would always control the circumstances. She shuddered at the thought of being forced into a marriage with some smelly old man, where she would likely be a third or fourth wife – which meant serving the more senior wives as a scullery maid, doing all the dirtiest tasks, and waiting hand and foot on those illiterate sows.

So it was with grave trepidations that she was returning home: twenty-six years old, highly educated, unmarried, career-minded and independent.

A perfect recipe for unending misery.

RIYADH

Trevor began breathing normally as he ran his fingers over the fifty cellophane-wrapped packets of 1000-Euro bills, each packet containing one-hundred bills - €5,000,000 in all. His mind did a quick calculation at the current exchange rate, which came to US$7 million – in cash. *Unmarked, untraceable, untaxable, invisible cash*, he thought. But what brought him to a full stop and made his hands tremble was the small, black velvet folio in the briefcase. For it held twenty large diamonds, each in its own individual see-through pouch. He could only imagine what they were worth, but it had to dwarf the amount of cash in front of him.

And then there was the terse, cryptic, unsigned memo that accompanied this fortune, printed on the heavy, cream-colored stationery of the Indo-Suez Bank. It read:

> "To the Committee:
>
> HRH insisted that this payment be made in-Kingdom to his representatives in this manner. They will have a detailed receipt bearing his signature upon delivery to them. HRH has determined that the facility must be expanded to accommodate the increased number of expected arrivals, and wishes the committee to address this issue and the attendant increased expense. He has asked that expansion be completed during the final phase of the plans, and that the increased expense be factored in.
>
> Rashid-Ali al-Suwaiket
> Executive Vice President & Chief Operating Officer"

"HRH"? His Royal Highness. That had to be some very senior member of the Saudi royal family – at a minimum one of the senior princes, or maybe even the king himself. Now he had a decision to make, a life-altering choice: he could turn in the swag to the hotel management and pray he hadn't already crossed some invisible line that could cost him his life or liberty. What if even just *knowing* about this would put his life in jeopardy? Who were those men in the elevator, and why were they here? Were any security cameras in that elevator?

"HRH"? Could it possibly be Crown Prince Mohammed bin Salman, "MBS", that crude, murderous psychopath? Oh, my God. That fact alone would make this thing a life-threatening proposition. And then it dawned on him that once it was discovered the briefcase was missing, all hell would break loose in the hotel. Every exit would be sealed while the Saudi secret police tore apart every room in the place, and woe be unto whoever they found in possession of the loot belonging to HRH – whoever *he* was. Trevor was deeply torn – should he just leave the briefcase in the lobby, where it could be found? And throw away the one chance to live his dream?

He hurriedly packed a suitbag, grabbed his checkbooks, wallet and the briefcase.

When he cautiously opened his door, he checked the hallway to see if Manny was at his usual station at the end of the hallway. It was deserted and quiet. He quickly eased the door shut and went down the emergency stairs two-at-a-time to a side-street exit. Everything seemed normal when he slipped off into the night and hailed a taxi some two blocks away.

Trevor checked into the Marriott Riyadh, on the other side of the city, and when comfortably ensconced in his room turned on the television. A special news report dominated the airwaves: The Al Khozama Hotel was under total lockdown due to a bomb threat. Saudi special security forces and police had ordered all guests to vacate their rooms and submit to full body searches while the rooms upstairs were being searched. A bomb scare? Now that was a sound and credible cover story. But it had all the earmarks of Crown Prince Mohammed's *modus operandi*.

He had escaped by a whisker. Now that the die was cast, he had to measure every step, weigh every option, think through as many potential consequences as he could imagine. One misstep could be fatal. But there could be no turning back, for what would he be returning to? Everything about his present life – *everything* – suggested a man who was about to be swallowed up by a sorry mediocrity.

This was it. How many people ever get a chance like this?

This was it. This was his big chance to be, finally, free to live the life of his dreams.

If he could get out of Saudi Arabia alive.

RIYADH

The daunting task was now clearly before Trevor: Finding a way to get out of Saudi with the money and jewels without raising any suspicions. Because going forward, every day spent in the Kingdom was a day in which his life would be in danger. His quasi-indentured status with the law firm, which had sponsored his entry into the country, allowed him one paid trip back to the US each year, but thus far he had only used them to vacation in the Canary Islands and London. As an only child, there was no family for him to return to see; only his father was living, retired and repatriated back to the Blue Mountains of Jamaica, among his kinsmen. And returning to New York – rich as Croesus - so soon after his ignominious departure would raise too many suspicions. So he was in hard reality a man with nowhere to go. He thought of Zurich, London, Cape Town, the South of France for a few years of anonymity before he rounded back to the States, leaving a cold trail behind him. He realized that he could go anywhere in the world, preferably some country that had no tax treaty with the U.S.; only a fool would report *all* of his expat bounty to the IRS. This money would never come onshore. He had a law school buddy who had been rotated to Hong Kong by Citibank for three years. When the three-year posting was ending, the bank tried to bring him back to the States, but he jumped ship and signed on with a large Hong Kong brokerage firm. He only paid U.S. income tax on such non-exempt portion of his salary as he chose; the first $100,000 was tax-exempt by law. Uncle Sam never found out about any of his side income and real estate investments in Thailand, Bali and London because that money remained offshore and for all official purposes did not exist.

But this was getting too far ahead of matters. At the moment, his highest priority was plotting a foolproof way out of Saudi with his windfall wealth.

He would have to invent some emergency, a reason to leave on short notice without revealing to anyone that he was never coming back. Or he could plan a weekend trip to Bahrain or Dubai, as many Saudis and guest workers did, where they could find alcohol and entertainment, and take it from there. The biggest problem was that the law firm was holding his passport as security in exchange for giving him his Igama, a work-permit, which was the custom for guest workers in the Kingdom. He could travel to the emirates on his Igama, but nowhere else without his U.S. passport. His sponsor – the law firm – had to approve his exit visa before he could leave the country. It was a delicate, dicey maneuver, and it had to be done in such a way that no suspicions would be aroused.

A soft knocking on the door so startled him that he leapt from the chair, scurrying to conceal the briefcase under his bed. His heart thundered as he quietly eased to the door and peered through the peephole.

It was only a tiny housekeeper, dressed in hotel livery. He exhaled heavily and opened the door.

"Please, sir, will you be needing anything from room service this evening, sir?" he said, smiling and bowing. "Do you need your bed turned down, sir?"

"No, thanks," Trevor replied, as a wave of relief washed over him.

"Yes, sir, thank you, sir, good evening, sir," he said, bowing deeply.

I can't live like this, Trevor thought. Yet practical considerations, coolly and soberly planned, had to be worked out. Hard, cold cash was fungible, yet he dared not spend any of it in-Kingdom just yet; things were much too hot at the moment. Taking any of the diamonds to be appraised inside the country was completely out of the question. He did not know their provenance, and those in the high-end jewelry business would almost certainly be on the lookout for them. So he had to hide the money and jewels in a safe place to which only he would have access until he was ready to make his break. His first stop would be Antwerp, the major diamond exchange in Europe, where no one would be asking any questions. A safe deposit box in Saudi was unwise, as the government had no restraints on violating the privacy of any non-royal in the country, especially westerners.

For the first time he realized just how isolated and alone he was. There was literally no one in the entire country that he could trust. *This is going to be a solo flight,* he whispered to himself.

RIYADH

The next morning found Trevor up before daybreak after a fitful, sleepless night. He had to deal first with the question of where he could safely stash his loot when he left for his office. For want of a better idea, he simply put it in the hotel room's wall safe for temporary safekeeping, then hung the "Do Not Disturb" notice on the doorknob.

Projecting an air of normality would come easily to him at the office. He was invisible to the dozen Saudi lawyers and their staff. When the other attorneys did interact with him, it was in much the same way as a master did with the hired help: genuine, unmasked condescension. They had also dumped the tasks of office management on him, a particularly degrading chore and imposition, especially for someone with his blue-chip pedigree. He might as well have been a tea-boy or messenger, but he had to swallow his pride, knuckle his head and take it. He was well-paid under his contract, but he could never aspire to equity partnership, where the real money was made. The fact that he could now buy and sell anybody in that office was a sobering thought, one that impelled him to keep his head down and his mouth shut, to check any impulse to express the slightest change of attitude from yesterday morning, before things had happened.

The doorman at the Marriott flagged him a taxi, and he went straightaway back to the Al Khozama Hotel to fetch his car from the garage.

Things had seemingly returned to normal at the hotel, but he suspected that surveillance cameras were recording all movement in the huge, high-ceilinged lobby. He walked purposefully to the elevator banks and went up to his apartment to pick up fresh clothing and personal effects. When he opened the door, he could see no evidence of a search, but found a sealed letter on his desk addressed to him personally. It was from the Saudi Police, Special

Tactical Unit. Without more, he turned on his heel, rushed from the room, and again hustled down the emergency stairs to the underground garage.

Usually, exiting the hotel garage was quick and easy, but there appeared to be some holdup ahead, as the line of cars in the exit line was stopped. Sensing trouble, Trevor slipped the unopened letter from his inner jacket pocket and slid it among the maps and other papers in the glovebox of his little BMW 300. Then he saw what was transpiring and felt droplets of cold sweat dripping from his armpit: the Saudi Special Police were ordering drivers out of their cars so that the cars could be searched. *Oh, shit,* he thought. He had no idea what was in the letter he had just picked up, or what these thugs might do if they found it. The Pakistani mercenaries were roughnecks, renowned and hired for their brutality.

Two of them approached his car and waved him out. They opened all four doors and popped the trunk, which contained nothing but a mesh bag of soiled laundry and a roadside emergency kit. His briefcase was opened, but it only contained legal papers and correspondence. His heart leaped up into his throat when one of the policemen opened the glovebox, but after seeing nothing but the usual bric-a-brac, he quickly closed it. These men seemed to know exactly what they were looking for. One of them held out a tray and demanded that Trevor empty his pockets and remove his jacket, while the other one patted him down.

"What is your occupation?" his searcher asked.

"I'm an attorney with the law firm of Fahad and Associates," he replied.

"What is your nationality?"

"American."

"What are you doing in this hotel?"

"I live here in one of the residence apartments."

"Where were you last evening?"

"I was working late last night, and when I came back here the place was under lockdown, so I spent the night in another hotel," he lied.

"Which hotel?"

Now Trevor was cornered. At all costs he had to steer them away from the Marriott, so he blurted out the first place that came to mind.

"The Ritz-Carlton," he said firmly, instantly realizing his gaffe.

The questioner turned to his colleague and spoke to him tersely, both men nodded some sort of agreement, and Trevor was waved through.

When he arrived at his office building, his shirt was soaked with sweat – and not from the searing heat. He was relieved that he had passed one test, but with so much money at stake – and the fact that it belonged to a certain Saudi royal – meant that this ugly business was not going away.

He parked his car in the underground garage and immediately hailed a taxi back to the Marriott. Within five minutes he had gone up to the room, emptied the contents of the safe back into the briefcase and hurried downstairs to take a taxi back to his office, where he checked out online.

In the solitude of his office, with the door closed, he ripped open the letter. It read:

"Dear Sir: Please contact Captain Osama Siddique at your earliest convenience at our headquarters building."

There was an address and telephone number below.

Fear slithered through his entrails like a snake.

Oh, shit, he thought. *What the fuck is this?*

WASHINGTON, D.C.

"How the fuck does anybody just 'lose' 80 million Euros in cash and diamonds? How? Can somebody explain that to me?" Robert Perkins demanded in a tense, heated, near-whisper. This elderly, tall, balding man in a dark suit, with his fierce, bird-of-prey, killer eyes, scanned the table from its head.

The three other men at the table, clearly intimidated, looked at the speaker, then each other, and shrugged helplessly.

The four sat alone in the private Pershing Room at the Army & Navy Club, overlooking Farragut Square in Washington, a mere three blocks from The White House.

"This looks and smells like an inside job to me," he said. "Typical of what happens when you deal on this level with the fucking Arabs. I've never trusted the bastards, but we have to tolerate them. I don't for one second believe that cock-and-bull story of a fucking briefcase inadvertently left on an elevator. Of course, the Prince doesn't want to hear any of this, and he'll have to eventually be paid, but in our own good time and on our terms. But can somebody explain why this meeting and delivery had to take place in the Kingdom? Didn't we decide that these meetings had to be held in London or Geneva or New York – where we wouldn't draw any attention? Whose bright idea was this – and why wasn't I informed?"

"Well, Mr. Perkins," began one of the men tentatively, "through his attorney, the Prince demanded that we meet in the Kingdom. He wanted to demonstrate that security could be ensured there, that he had everything under control. He insisted--"

"We don't take orders from those sand-niggers, no matter what they call themselves," snapped Perkins. "Couldn't somebody have told him that there were logistical problems from our side? I mean, come on! Any credible lie would have sufficed, and we could have maintained airtight control."

"Mr. Perkins," ventured one of the men hopefully, "we've been advised that the Prince is furious. He's put on a secret full-court press in the Kingdom, including an offer through the back channels of a sizable reward for critical information leading to whoever is behind the heist. Apparently the elevator security cameras were down for servicing when the briefcase disappeared."

The only man at the table who knew the Prince's true identity - and who interfaced with him - was Perkins.

Perkins snorted his contempt. "As if somebody having knowledge would voluntarily come forward? That is pure insanity, and it would be the kiss of death for anyone who did. But the money is the least of it. Gentlemen, you know that we're finishing construction of a new, state-of-the-art center in the Empty Quarter of Saudi Arabia, deep in the Saudi desert. It is currently in the completion and trim stages. A facility that will be completely invisible to everyone but us, and escape-proof. Was the Gemini Project Completion Report in that briefcase?"

"We understand that it was, sir," said one of the men.

"All right," said Perkins, quietly. "I'll get word back to the Prince that we're sending in one of our crack special ops teams to get to the bottom of this. I don't trust those goddamned dune-coons as far as I can throw this fucking building. I will convey to him that our people are being dispatched immediately to, ah, assist him."

"Yes, sir."

"And I would remind all of you that this entire project is above and beyond top secret, and that we don't answer to anyone but our sponsors. The president himself and the head of the CIA have no official knowledge or authority over us or what we do. Let me be clear: At the end of the day, the money is not nearly as critical as the information. It's a drop in the bucket, but we want it back anyway. The point here is that we have never – *never* – had one security breach since this project was established twelve years ago. And we definitely cannot allow it now, with so much at stake. Gentlemen, I don't have to tell you that the future of the United States and all of mankind hangs in the balance. *That* should be motivation enough."

Perkins immediately rose and left the room without another word.

The three other men sat in total silence for several very long minutes.

———〜〜ᗢᘓᕮᗣᘰᗢ〜〜———

Perkins sat in his den, reflecting on this latest glitch. His thoughts turned to his former boss, long-term benefactor and inspiration: Allen Dulles, the founding father of what would become the CIA. He was the longest-serving Director of the CIA and a god to Perkins, who served as his Deputy Director, Aide-de-Camp, hatchetman and facilitator for over a decade. Dulles's singular vision, forged by the immediate aftermath of World War II and the ensuing Cold War, required operations completely without oversight by any person or body. He was the quintessential Cold Warrior.

Perkins, not yet thirty, cut his teeth in Iran with Operation Ajax in 1953, when Dulles orchestrated the first U.S. covert action to overthrow a foreign government during peacetime. Perkins helped install the treacherous and authoritarian Shah of Iran after driving out a popular and democratically-elected prime minister. Rumors of the nationalization of the Anglo-Iranian Oil Company and of Soviet influence had precipitated this "regime change", the very first to be effected in peacetime – and certainly not the last. They were just getting started.

Perkins sat at his elbow in 1954, when Dulles masterminded the coup d'etat in Guatemala, overthrowing the democratically-elected president and installing the military dictatorship of Carlos Castillo Armas, the first in a series of U.S-backed military dictators there. Dulles sat on the board of the United Fruit Company, so he faced little opposition in unilaterally declaring "vital U.S. interests" to be at stake.

The U-2 Spy Program was another Dulles brain-child born of the Cold War. It was enormously informative until 1960, when CIA pilot Francis Gary Powers was shot down from 70,000 feet by a Soviet missile. The embarrassment to Eisenhower was particularly stinging because he had been deep in negotiations with Khrushchev over arms control. To protect his boss, Perkins took full blame for the incident, sparing Dulles.

With the full blessing of Dulles and as a favor to the Belgians and the French, Perkins arranged the assassination of Patrice Lumumba in the Congo, on January 17, 1961, three days before John F. Kennedy would be sworn in as President. Lumumba's attraction to and courtship with the Soviet Union had to be nipped in the bud, and before Kennedy took office and could possibly stop this elimination.

"Regime change" as a viable and acceptable geo-political option entered the common lexicon because of the quintessential Cold Warrior, Allen Dulles.

But the charmed life of Allen Dulles would take a decidedly different trajectory after the disastrous Bay of Pigs invasion of Cuba in April of 1961. And so would that of his faithful and loyal squire, Robert Perkins.

RIYADH

Trevor murmured his greeting to the male receptionist at the firm, Rashid, and unobtrusively slipped into his office.

The first order of business was finding a safe hiding place in his office for the briefcase and its contents. He did not want it in his own individual office, but recent maintenance work – which, as office manager, he had had to supervise –gave him an idea. The file room had recently been re-configured and expanded, and the workmen had installed a new dropped ceiling and fluorescent lighting.

Early that afternoon, when everyone was out for midday break, he got a stepladder from the facilities closet, took it to the file room, and closed and locked the door. Gingerly, he climbed upon the ladder in a far corner of the windowless room, pushed up one of the ceiling panels and surveyed the narrow crawl space. It was perfect. He could stash the briefcase in a darkened corner up there, away from the light fixtures, where no one would ever have reason to look. And if on the off-chance someone did, it could not be tied to him. That mission was accomplished.

The presiding partner of the firm, Mr. Fahad, had recently hired his twenty-six-year-old daughter, Souheir, to work as a paralegal in the firm. Under Saudi law, women are allowed to work directly for a male relative. She had just returned from New York City, where she had been a student at NYU. She would show up in the mornings with her father, dressed in the usual abaya, a black sack with a veil, and immediately change into jeans and a sweatshirt. Without that accursed veil, she revealed her radiant beauty: flashing dark eyes, smooth olive skin, long, flowing black hair, topping off a lean, fit gym body. Yet she averted her eyes whenever she approached anyone – except Trevor. To him, she alternately revealed a smoldering, defiant resentment, or a desperate, unspoken plea. He couldn't figure it out, except that she was one very unhappy young woman. She never spoke unless spoken to first. He wondered what was going on behind those dark, expressive eyes. In another time and place, he would have long since made his move on her. But that was totally out of the question here; unmarried sex could bring the death penalty.

Souheir almost never left the office for midday break, preferring instead to spend it in a locked conference room with her books and cell phone. Today, she opened the door after an hour, and for the first time ever came to his office doorway.

"Mr. Osborne?" she spoke meekly. "I have some slack time and wonder if you need any help."

Surprised, he remained seated and cautiously regarded her. "Please call me Trevor. And since you ask, I actually do need some documents indexed for the Dhahran Pipeline deal. I'll bundle them with the instructions. No rush. Okay?"

"Yes, thank you," she said, finally smiling. "I'll have them in your mailbox tomorrow morning."

⟿∿∘ᘓᕑᘏᘓᕑᘎ∘∿⟾

He felt greatly relieved, which emboldened him to finally telephone the police captain who had summoned him. His stomach churned with anxiety when he dialed the number and listened to the phone ringing. On the twentieth ring, it was finally answered.

"Captain Siddique's office," said a sharp, clipped, Pakistani voice on the other end.

"Yes, I received a letter today asking me to contact Captain Siddique, so I'm trying to reach him."

"Captain Siddique is not available at the moment. Call back later."

"Well, sir, I think this might be very important, so perhaps you could tell me the best time to phone him, and I'd like to leave my name along with a message."

"Call back later," ordered the rude voice, hanging up without any hint of common courtesy.

Trevor decided to go on a bold offensive instead of ducking and dodging in the shadows. *Don't wait for anyone to come looking for you,* he told himself. Now that his bounty was safely stashed he could construct a credible alibi or two, feign ignorance and innocence, and imply that the blame lay elsewhere.

So he was not expected when he presented himself late that afternoon at the severe headquarters of the Special Tactical Unit of the Saudi Police, near the famous Red Palace, and asked to see Captain Siddique.

"Have you an appointment?" asked the sharp-faced, Pakistani policeman at the front-desk.

"No, sir. I tried to arrange one over the telephone but it couldn't be done. So I came over as quickly as I could."

"Captain Siddique cannot see you without an appointment. It is quite impossible."

Trevor presented the letter to him, saying "This was left in my apartment at the Al Khozama Hotel last evening."

"Did you say the Al Khozama?" asked the guard.

"Yes, sir."

"Wait a moment," he said, suddenly concerned. He picked up the telephone, dialed, and spoke quietly into it. Then to Trevor, "Please take a seat. Someone will escort you up to his office shortly."

Trevor felt weakness in his knees when he was ushered into Captain Siddique's large corner office and found not just the captain, sitting behind his desk, but two other uniformed officers standing next to him, one on either side. He immediately recognized them as the two guards who had been standing outside the elevator on the penthouse floor the previous night. *Oh, fuck*, he thought, *will they remember me?*

"Please have a seat, Mr. Osborne," said the captain, motioning to a chair before his desk.

Trevor sat down, his heart in his mouth, affecting a casualness he was far from feeling.

"I take it you know what this is about," said the captain.

"No, sir," said Trevor, "I'm afraid I don't."

"No?" said the captain. "Then perhaps you can tell us of your whereabouts last night after seven o'clock."

"Of course," replied Trevor amiably. "I had dinner at La Trattoria on Al Olaya Boulevard, and I left there at about eight and walked back to the Al Khozama, where I live. I stopped at the front desk to get my mail, and went up to my room to pick some things up before going back to my office to finish up some legal work on an important matter. I took a taxi over because it was quicker. When I got back to the hotel around ten, I couldn't get in because of a lockdown. Somebody outside told me it was a bomb threat. So, I went over to the Marriott, checked in, and spent the night there."

Captain Siddique leafed through a file before him. He said nothing, and Trevor forced himself to stay visibly cool and unruffled. Finally, he spoke.

"The security cameras at the Al Khozama show you at the front desk last night. But they do not show you leaving. You also told security this morning that you stayed last night at the Ritz Carlton, not the Marriott."

Trevor knew that he had to keep his head and wits about him now; this encounter could prove fatal if he slipped up.

"Well, after I left my room, I took the elevator straight down to the garage to get some files from my car, then I came out by the garage side-exit because it was closer. I may have mentioned the Ritz this morning, but I always get these different hotels confused," he said, smiling and shrugging helplessly. "Check with the front desk at the Marriott. I was there, and I have a receipt for the stay." Then, after a long pause, "Can you please tell me what this is about? I don't know anything about any bomb threat. I'm just an American corporate attorney with a law firm."

"We're asking the questions at this moment," snapped the captain. "Now tell me, when you went up to your place last night, did you notice anything or anyone? Was anyone on that elevator with you?"

"Yes. There were five, maybe six western businessmen. I'd never seen them before. I forgot to push the button for my floor because two of them suddenly started fighting in the elevator before they were separated by the others. I rode up with them to the private penthouse level, then rode down to my floor."

"Did you get off on the private floor?"

"No. Why would I?"

"When these men got off the elevator, did they leave anything behind?"

"No, not that I recall."

"A briefcase, perhaps?"

"No," he said firmly. "I didn't see one." And then after a long pause, "Is there anything else, sir?"

"We will investigate this matter further and we may wish to talk to you again, but at the moment you are free to go." Then, "Do you have a business card? We need to be able to reach you in the future."

Trevor slid his card across the desk. "Can you please tell me what this is about, captain?"

Captain Siddique's flat, lifeless eyes gave away nothing.

"No," he snapped.

JEDDAH, SAUDI ARABIA

Trevor decided to spend the next Saudi weekend – Thursday and Friday – at the beach in Jeddah, on the western coast hard by the Red Sea. He caught the two-hour commuter flight to Jeddah on Wednesday afternoon, and checked into the Hyatt Regency there.

Thursday morning found him sitting in a sunny, seaside café. Jeddah, the commercial center of the Kingdom, is viewed as the most open city, but this is a relative assessment. Public bathing – in a beachfront city of four million - is prohibited unless one is fully clothed. Private beach clubs get around his problem, but it is not exactly the beach vacation any westerner would have in mind.

But he had come to Jeddah on a reconnaissance mission, one far more important than the pleasures of sun and sand.

After breakfast, he ambled down to the waterfront marina on the Red Sea. Fishing boats, diving and deep-sea fishing charters, and a raft of huge pleasure boats sat at rest in long rows. One needed prior authorization to access these piers. He inquired at a visitor's booth about fishing and possibly scuba diving, and was sent down the dock to speak with the owner of a charter service. The owner was not present, but his manager, a grizzled, weathered black American, was there.

"Excuse me, but I'm looking for a Samir Hamza. Do you know when he'll be back?"

"Whaddya need, young bro?"

"I'd like to do some deep-sea fishing, and maybe some wreck-diving in the Red Sea. What do you offer in the way of half-day fishing trips?"

"We do half days, but only with a minimum of four guests at $250 a head. Half days run from 8:00 a.m. to noon, and from 1:00 p.m. to five. If we don't get the head count, we don't go out. Ain't cost effective."

"Can I rent a boat for a day's sail? You know, like a private day charter?"

The man laughed, rather like a donkey-bray of derision. "Tell me, bro, what do you know about the Saudi Coast Guard?"

"Excuse me?"

"Oh, come on, dude, you ain't the first fool to consider swimming or floating outta this motherfucker."

Trevor immediately commenced a feeble protest, but the man cut him off.

"Listen, my man, they watch this fucking waterfront like hawks. They're always stopping and boarding boats for so-called random inspections. And they don't always stay in their territorial waters, either. Every few months or so you read about some young dummy trying to run away and getting caught. And some old ones, too. Forget it, man. Ain't worth getting' caught and dyin' in jail here."

Trevor flew back Riyadh the next evening, having answered one burning question about his exit plans.

WASHINGTON, D.C.

Robert Perkins leaned back in his desk chair and admired the view across the Potomac River from his sumptuous office high above Georgetown. The name on the manifest downstairs simply read "Vanguard Associates". He felt totally secure because he owned the building and held it through a limited liability company as the nominal owner. This gave him imprimatur to have the walls of his office steel-reinforced and fireproofed, and to have a walk-in safe and stand-alone e-mail server installed within. He had resolved to take no chances with security.

The meeting at the Army & Navy Club a week earlier had left him fretting about security elsewhere, namely in Saudi Arabia. He and his cohorts were planning a major move in a relatively supine country, where the royal family, through its networks of secret police and informants, maintained air-tight control over practically everything and everyone. In exchange, Perkins and his sponsors had pledged their fealty to the royal family in providing intelligence on terrorism, and on subversive and radical Islamic activity in the Kingdom. It was a comfortable *quid pro quo,* conducted completely outside of governmental channels, a true and genuine "meeting of the minds". Only one U.S. president, past or present, had ever been made generally aware of the work commissioned and supported by the sponsors: George Herbert Walker Bush. The disclosures were unspecific, but pointed enough to convey the overarching purpose, for even an ex-president needed plausible deniability. All of the others were deemed too unreliable – and likely too hostile to the mission – for any disclosure. The last thing the sponsors wanted was congressional or other government oversight. Even the $30 billion annually spent by the U.S. on CIA black projects required limited oversight by Congress. This project, however, was much too sensitive to be exposed in any way to a bunch of egomaniacal, two-bit elected officials whom the sponsors could buy with pocket-change. The sensitivity of the work mandated complete secrecy. Ex-president Jimmy Carter, who had heard vague whispers from the highest military circles, put it out that he wanted to be briefed, only to be completely stonewalled by this group. And there was nothing he could do about it.

The American people, thought Perkins, *are the most childlike – and childish – on this planet. They expect to be protected from all known and unknown hazards of the dangerous world we inhabit. This is a dirty business, and we protect them in ways they're too naïve to realize. Yet they expect someone, somehow, to protect them. From all terrors. And for the most part, they're too squeamish to comprehend just how it's done. The events of 9/11 precipitated the agenda and proved more fortuitous than anyone could have possibly imagined. Now we have a real casus belli, and the west can have no objection to it. Trying to discreetly keep Dick Cheney on the reservation – while keeping him completely in the dark - has proven quite difficult, despite all the warnings from our sponsors. But he had to have his expedition in Iraq, a stupid and futile exercise in ego and resource control. And look how that turned out. In many ways it proved to be just the distraction we needed. No, this time it would be totally different.*

But more pressing matters were at hand. Perkins had received a confidential report from the New York office on a man identified as a "person of interest" in Saudi Arabia: one Trevor Derek Osborne, an American attorney working in the Kingdom who happened to be on the premises when the item in question disappeared. Clandestine searches of his apartment in the Al Khozama Hotel and his office by Saudi secret police had turned up nothing, but this was no disincentive; if he was, in fact, involved, he would certainly be cagey enough to bury the loot far from his usual haunts. So, the next step was to shadow his every move, to determine the identities of any persons with whom he associated, and to put them under surveillance as well. Meanwhile, Perkins had surreptitiously ordered similar action on all of the men who met in the hotel on that fateful night. If this was indeed an inside job – as Perkins suspected – they would eventually identify the culprit.

He found the report on Trevor most illuminating. The son and only child of Jamaican immigrants, both civil servants in Brooklyn, his mother died of cancer his freshman year of college, and his father never remarried. He took early retirement and moved back to Jamaica. There was nothing remarkable about his middle-class upbringing or his educational pedigree: Stuyvesant High School, Amherst College, Harvard Law School. Clerked for a federal appeals judge in New York, went on to the premier, white-shoe, Wall Street firm of Milbank Tweed. Toiled seven years in the firm's corporate sector before being axed for his role as a witness in a sexual assault case, divorced by his wife, just another washed-up, worn out, dime-a-dozen New York associate with a great shoeshine. *You can stand on any street-corner in New York, spit, and hit five or six such guys,* Perkins thought. *There are countless identical stories in Manhattan, but nobody ever hears about all the losers required to validate the handful of lucky lottery winners. The quintessential zero-sum game writ large.*

Perkins was confident and sure of his judgment of character based on a written profile, without ever having met a person, and this he felt his strongest suit. He could sense human motivation, mind-set, and proclivity simply by putting himself into that person's shoes and asking, "What would I do under these circumstances?" It was an uncanny sixth sense that rarely played him false.

I knew his type at Yale and afterward. Here's a striver, an immigrants' kid who is thoroughly invested, emotionally and otherwise, in one American Dream, the New York BigLaw Sweepstakes. He leaves Manhattan, broke, broken, divorced and embittered, thought Perkins. *Those are the reasons he's in Saudi, because no sane person with real choices in this life would voluntarily embrace that dreadful existence. No, westerners go there for just one thing: money. And if Osborne just happened upon that briefcase, what would his likely reaction be? Would he see it as a form of redemption, his just desserts, a form of payback, a way out of his dead-end circumstances, a ticket to his dreams? With his mile-high ego? Yes, most definitely. And would he put his sorry life at risk for it? Absolutely. But the bottom-line question would be this: Would he have the sheer nerve, the will, the smarts and the guts to pull it off?*

What would he have to lose – other than that sorry-ass life?

RIYADH

While the meeting at the special police headquarters was unnerving, Trevor felt a tidal wave of relief wash over him after he left the building. *So far, so good,* he thought. But he was on their radar now, and clearly in the danger zone. He initially thought that the two security guards did not recognize him, but decided to assume the worst – that they did – and operate on that assumption going forward without expressly stating it. With the cash and diamonds safely hidden, he could afford to take his time to cautiously and deliberately plan his escape.

So for the next week he returned to his lugubrious routine, largely keeping to himself and seeming to devote undivided attention to his work. But concentrating on anything other than his nascent plan was all but impossible. He sensed that the privacy of his apartment and office had been violated, that they might even be bugged, but who could he complain to?

He also sensed that escaping would be far more difficult and dangerous than he'd thought. Because Saudi Passport Control had almost certainly been alerted and would be on the lookout for him if he tried to sneak out of the Kingdom.

Just how difficult hit home when he returned to his apartment after dinner one evening, planning to take a short nap before returning to the office to finish up some outstanding matters. As he plumped up a pillow, he discovered underneath a sealed letter on hotel stationery. When he tore it open, he found the following message scrawled on a single unsigned sheet of hotel letterhead:

"Dear Mr. Osborne: Please be careful. They watching you."

Trevor felt a jarring sensation, a feeling of having been violated in some way. Who could this be from? Did someone in the hotel see him slip away on the night in question? Was this a set-up, a trap of some kind to have an informant gain his confidence? *This,* thought Trevor, *is what gives a police state its extraordinary power: mortal fear and a distrust of everyone – no exceptions."*

Whoever left the note in his bed would surface again in some guise or other. Until that time, Trevor would do nothing to determine who it might be. But in the meantime, he would play it straight and employ a gambit that would almost certainly test security and force his overseers to tip their hand.

RIYADH

Sitting alone in the anteroom of the firm's presiding partner, Dr. Rashid Fahad, was akin to awaiting an audience with some dignitary. All Saudi attorneys pretentiously called themselves "Dr." – undoubtedly because the diplomas read "Juris Doctor" – and all had had training in the U.S. or the U.K. But Trevor was calm, rested and relaxed, giving away nothing in his demeanor. The male secretary in the room ignored him until Dr. Fahad buzzed and asked that Trevor be sent in.

Dr. Fahad, a nattily-dressed, sixtyish man in an Armani suit and expensive Bally loafers, affected a courtly demeanor that disguised the rapacity of a hungry wolf. He had been sent at government expense to Yale Law School, with post-graduate work at Johns Hopkins.

His twenty-six-year-old daughter, Souheir, was just exiting her father's office as Trevor was going in. She betrayed no emotion and did not speak to him. She seemed as though she wanted to merge into the wallpaper and disappear.

Trevor vividly recalled an evening in the office a week earlier, when he was awaiting the usual e-mails from New York. During the day, he always worked with his office door closed, but in the evenings, when he was frequently there alone, he opened his door to the outer office. That evening he was heading to the copy room when heard Dr. Fahad, behind his own closed door, barking loudly and angrily at someone. Then he heard Souheir, shrieking and sobbing, begging and pleading. They were speaking Arabic, which Trevor did not understand. But he intuited, by the tone and pitch and emotion in those voices, that something unpleasant was being inflicted on the young woman. He eased back into his office and quietly closed his door

Thereafter, Souheir retreated into a sullen silence in the office, speaking only when spoken to. Trevor wondered what angry, rebellious thoughts reposed behind those beautiful, smoldering dark eyes.

———— ᴡᴏᴄᴇᴏᴏᴇᴏᴏᴡ ————

"So," said Dr. Fahad, smiling, "you wish to spend some weekend time in Bahrain, yes?"

"Yes," said Trevor wryly. "I've heard all the great things about it, so I thought I'd go and see for myself since I'm planning to be in this neighborhood for a while."

"You are driving? Then be very careful. Every weekend the checkpoints catch dozens of inebriated Saudi fools in their big German autos coming back from Bahrain."

"So noted, sir," said Trevor, grinning. "I'm just planning to have one or two cocktails."

"Tell Samir to file the exit visa permit," he said pleasantly. Then, pausing, he asked, "So how are things with you, Trevor? You're very quiet but efficient. The partners respect your judgment and advice, and we are pleased that you chose to join us. Is there anything you need?"

"I'm fine. Things are fine. Solitude fosters self-examination," he said cryptically.

"Good. Let me know straightaway if you need anything."

The moment his door closed, Dr. Fahad picked up the phone and punched in a number, his smile gone, his face tight and grim.

———— ᴡᴏᴄᴇᴏᴏᴇᴏᴏᴡ ————

Trevor needed human, interpersonal contact, anything to take his thoughts away from his oppressive concerns. He felt his head ready to explode from the anxiety and fear. So he left a note at the concierge station on his hotel floor for Manny. He wanted to play some tennis on the hotel rooftop that evening, a pleasant diversion of perhaps an hour away from his own dark thoughts.

THE ARABIAN DESERT

The drive from Riyadh to Al-Khobar, in the eastern province, was a pleasant four-hour trip through the desert along Highway 40. There were no cities or towns along the route, only service stations with mini-marts spaced at twenty-mile intervals. The traffic was steady, as many expats were heading to Bahrain for the "Saudi weekend" – Thursday and Friday – along with Saudi pleasure seekers, all looking for alcohol, music and other delights.

For Trevor, the trip was liberating – out on the open road, singing along with the satellite radio Golden Oldies station, his worries and cares forgotten for two short days in anticipation of booze, food and, if he got really lucky, maybe some female company.

He would soon approach a series of checkpoints, where his papers would be thoroughly scrutinized, and both the car and his physical person possibly searched for contraband. This would be the acid test, the sole purpose of the trip: to determine whether or not – and to what extent – he had become a "person of interest" in the Kingdom. He was fully prepared to answer any questions with a bland, wide-eyed, "Who me?" faux innocence, and they could tear the car apart if they wanted. He had checked every nook and cranny of the car, just to be certain that nothing had been planted in it so that he would be clean in every way on this excursion. He smiled as he likened himself to a sly velociraptor, checking the fences for an escape route.

About three hours into the trip, he pulled off at a service station and mini-mart to re-fuel and grab a Coke. He suddenly noticed a black SUV with black-out windows pull off behind him, but nobody got out; it simply sat there, as though waiting for something or someone. The anonymous letter slipped under his door at the hotel was never far from his mind, and he wondered if this might be a part of any surveillance.

He decided to test his theory. As he pulled out of the station, the black SUV also began moving toward the exit. He had not observed anyone getting in or out of the car. About a mile down the highway, he checked in his rearview mirror and there it was, maybe a half-mile behind. The black SUV shadowed him for the next twenty miles, hanging back just far enough so as not to be obvious, but keeping him well within their sight. When he sped up, so did the SUV; when he slowed, it did also. He decided to have some fun with whoever was back there.

Approaching the next service stop, he suddenly and without warning swung into the parking lot and waited. Sure enough, the black SUV slowed and turned in as well. Again, no one exited the vehicle; whoever it was just sat and waited. He went into the mart, never taking his eyes off the SUV behind his sunglasses. Inside the mart he took his sweet time: he bought a slice of lousy pizza, browsed the newspaper racks, just killed a little time, never taking his eyes from his car. Then he went back out, got in, and headed slowly for the exit. Suddenly he made a hard left turn onto the highway, hit the accelerator, and zoomed back in the direction of Riyadh at over 100 mph. *They wouldn't be expecting this move*, he thought, all the while staring at the rearview mirror to see the reaction. Sure enough, a few miles down the highway, he espied the SUV, about a mile behind, creeping back up on him.

Now came the fun part. He waited until the SUV closed to within two hundred yards and, again without warning, suddenly pulled a sharp U-turn and reversed direction, now heading back toward Bahrain. As he blew past the black SUV heading in the opposite direction, he was seized with the urge to roll down his window and tauntingly wave at the followers, but decided that such a deliberate provocation would be foolish in this place. He studied his mirror intently, waiting to see what they would do. At first the SUV slowed uncertainly, almost to a stop, and then continued on its way. They knew that they'd been spotted.

So one question was answered; yes, he was under surveillance. But the key question remained hanging over his head: Who was behind this, and what was at stake – other than his own life and liberty? And if Crown Prince Mohammed bin Salman was indeed the "HRH" in the bank documents, what would he do to an infidel American thief who had stolen millions from him?

Trevor shuddered at the prospect.

AL-KHOBAR, SAUDI ARABIA

Trevor was suddenly filled with regret and self-loathing as he approached the first of the seven checkpoints. That was an incredibly stupid thing he'd done back there with the tailing SUV. Now they knew that *he* was onto *them*, and it would only result in the tightening of the net that loosely circumscribed him. And these fuckers didn't bother with such troublesome details as probable cause, search and arrest warrants, due process of law or any of the other irksome features of western justice systems. If they were so inclined, he could be locked up and held indefinitely on mere unfounded suspicion.

Goddammit! What had he been thinking when he impulsively pulled that boneheaded stunt back there? He should have ignored it and played dumb. And why didn't he note the numbers on the license plate? Surely that might have been helpful at some point.

At the first checkpoint his Igama and exit papers were quickly reviewed by heavily-armed border patrol guards and he was peremptorily waved through. This perfunctory procedure was repeated at the next five checkpoints, which only aroused his curiosity. He was waiting for the unpleasantry and, sure enough, the seventh and last checkpoint was where he encountered it. The armed guards, guns drawn, waved him to pull over to a special facility, ordered him out of the car and demanded that he empty his pockets and submit to a full body pat-down while they searched every nook and cranny of the car – even going so far as to open the hood and to send an inspector under the car to search for hidden contraband. They opened his weekend bag and pulled out all of his clothing and personal effects onto a table, where they went through every stitch, including his dopp kit. He had been prescient enough not to carry condoms with him, as this would have served as a real provocation – an intent to debauch Muslim womanhood.

Then they did something that totally jarred him, even though he was expecting it. They took his wallet from the tray, pulled out all the currency, and took it into the checkpoint center for inspection. He knew that they were painstakingly checking every Euro bill to see if the serial numbers matched the money that was missing, and because he had not touched that money, he also knew that he was in the clear on at least this score.

"*Motherfuckers,*" he thought, flashing his blandest smile. "*Sonsabitches.*"

They held him up there for nearly an hour as he stood in the blazing midday heat watching other vehicles being routinely waved through. Finally, a high-ranking officer, ugly as sin, approached him and asked why he was going to Bahrain. The man had a face like a hatchet and eyes like rusty nails; he scarcely seemed human.

Trevor was all wide-eyed innocence. "Well, I haven't been out of the Kingdom in months, and I wanted to see what Bahrain is like," he explained. "I've never been."

"Would you object to coming inside and submitting to a cavity search?" the official asked sharply.

"No, not at all," replied Trevor mildly. "How long will it take?"

The officer turned the full force of his stare to Trevor, seeming to consider the next move, fixing that intense stare on him for a full thirty seconds. Then he handed back the stamped papers and announced that Trevor was free to go.

As he repacked his car, Trevor could feel that stare following him, burning two holes in his back.

If he had learned anything, it was that slipping away through Bahrain with his swag was a non-starter. Mission accomplished. Time to have some fun and then consider other escape routes. One thing was absolutely clear: He could not leave this accursed place empty-handed. After all, what did he have to go back to? What would he do? Where could he go? Yes, it was a huge risk he was taking, but what choice did he have?

WASHINGTON, D.C.

"The worst thing that could happen may very well have happened," declared Robert Perkins to the three men sitting at the conference table in his Georgetown office suite. "We could be looking at a major security breach, the first in the history of this project," he said, shifting from one to another with his feral, killer eyes.

The same three men who had met with him several days earlier at the Army-Navy Club were at the table, exhibiting an ease they were far from feeling.

Perkins continued. "It's not just the money. There was also a package containing the builder's progress and completion reports for the facility, the background considerations, its purpose and function. That should have been in the goddamned briefcase with the money and diamonds. And now that's missing, too."

"Mr. Perkins," meekly offered one of the men, "Our security team is in the air at this very moment. They'll be stopping in Frankfurt to refuel, and should be in-Kingdom by tonight."

"And therefore?" Perkins snapped in reply.

"Well, sir, I just mean to say that--"

"Listen, goddammit, I want no expense spared on this one. Whoever is behind this will never get out of the Kingdom alive. We're taking no chances, pulling out all the stops. I will not allow nearly twenty years of work to go down the fucking drain. And those closest to this problem will face serious consequences – *ultimate* consequences – if this doesn't get fixed immediately. Do I make myself clear?"

They knew exactly what he meant.

The three men, ashen-faced and sober, nodded gravely in unison.

Perkins abruptly stood, saying nothing more, indicating that the meeting was over.

RIYADH

Trevor eased his car into a space in the garage beneath his office building. It was early Saturday morning and he had just returned from Bahrain, surfeited with good food and copious drink, but once again anxious and deeply troubled by his predicament. He hated having to return to Saudi, but he had nowhere else to go. Going back to the Al Khozama Hotel would only have depressed him, especially since receiving the mysterious anonymous note there. Whenever he was at his residence quarters now he felt as though he was laboring under some watchful, invisible, unblinking giant eye, recording his every move, so he'd come directly to the office. The black SUV that had been trailing him on his way to Bahrain was never far from his mind, feeding his growing but abundantly justified paranoia.

He had bought with cash two new smartphones in Bahrain, and had programmed a whole new identity, such that he could use them to plot his escape from Saudi. He also purchased four prepaid, disposable "burner" phones, which could not be traced. He put this package up in the ceiling with the briefcase. If his old phone was seized, there would be nothing on it connecting him to the loot or his plans for an escape. Acting on a paranoid hunch, he had visited a security firm in Bahrain and requested that they inspect his car for any foreign devices.

They quickly found a small GPS transmitter, attached to the inside of his front fender. He asked that they leave it. He suspected that if it suddenly stopped emitting its signal, they would swoop down on him. So he resolved to keep it in place until he made his break for freedom.

Upstairs in his office he turned on his computer to review the emails that had come from the states over his long weekend, looking to get a head start on the coming week's workload. He reached for his phone and started. It was sitting askew on the cradle, certainly not the way he'd left it, and instantly he knew someone had been in his office. He felt personally violated. For now he realized that the phone had likely been bugged in his absence, and that every word he spoke was being heard by some unknown, uninvited ear. Thank God he had the new, secret phones.

But never far from his thoughts was the letter from the Saudi Special Police. Someone in the hotel was onto him, and in a very significant – and frightening – way. But who could it be? He had no real friends or acquaintances. He went to his office, he came back to the hotel, and for the most part kept entirely to himself. Occasionally he would go to the hotel gym and work out, or he'd play some pickup tennis with Manny at the rooftop courts, but that was it.

There was not one person in Saudi Arabia that he could really talk to.

———— ·⁓⊸◦◖◠◗◦◖◠◗◦⊷⁓· ————

Under a clear, black desert sky, still perspiring but filled with a nervous, kinetic energy, Trevor sat alone with Manny at the deserted rooftop tennis court, nursing a pitcher of Saudi Cooler, which was simply apple juice blended with seltzer. While his body cried out for a double-vodka martini, this beverage would have to do. They made small talk, mainly about Manny's eleven siblings back in Manila, and how he and his younger brother, Ferdie, were helping their mother by sending home monthly payments to support the family. Manny, usually enthusiastic and voluble, was uncharacteristically quiet, as though something was bothering him. He seemed to be searching for a way to unburden himself. Finally, Trevor asked, "Is something troubling you, Manny? You're awfully quiet tonight." Then, after a long pause, he said "You can share it with me."

Manny hesitated, but Trevor nodded, encouraging him. Haltingly, Manny began.

"Meester Osborne, you are lawyer, right?"

"Yes, I am. Why do you ask?"

"Please, don't tell nobody, okay?"

"Of course. This is just you and me talking, all right?"

"Yes, sir." He took a deep breath and began. "I come here with my little brother to help out my mother with my brothers and sisters. We got nothing back home, eleven kids, no father, never enough to eat, every day a struggle just to feed everybody. So we signed up to get work here."

"Go on," coaxed Trevor gently.

"It's my brother, sir. He having big problem."

"Where does he work?"

"At the Al Faisaliah Hotel, sir. He's a bellhop."

"And what is his problem?"

"The Bell Captain accuse him of stealing from customers. They investigating it and tell him he could go to jail. But he tell me he never take anything, that he see the Bell Captain stealing, but they blame him." Then he became plaintive. "Meester Osborne, Ferdie is good guy. He never take anything. I believe him. But if they lock him up, I have to stay here. I'm the oldest, and my job is taking care of the younger ones. I cannot leave him here alone."

"What would you have me do? I'm not licensed here, so I can't take any official action."

"Please, sir, maybe you could talk to somebody. You the only other person I know here. Please."

"Manny, I want to help, but I'm not sure how I can. But I have to ask you something. And I want you to tell me the truth. Remember the night of the bomb scare two weeks ago?"

"Yes, sir."

"Well, last week, someone – I don't know who – got into my room and slipped a note under my pillow. Did you see or hear anything on the floor? Do you know who might have done it?"

Manny stared fixedly at the ground. Trevor waited calmly. Finally, Manny raised his head, and his eyes locked with Trevor's penetrating stare.

"Sir, I am afraid. You won't tell nobody? Please?"

"Not a soul."

"I did it, sir."

"Why?"

"Because I see them – security – come to your room when you leave. They order me to keep quiet."

"I see. Tell me, Manny, where were you on the night of the bomb scare?"

Manny hesitated, his eyes filling with fear and dread, his voice dropping to a whisper. "They ask me to work a meeting up on penthouse floor," he whispered. "They send me down to front desk to pick up package from special courier. The package wasn't there. When I come back up, the meeting was over real quick and everybody gone. Then all hell break loose in hotel."

"What about the package? What happened to it?"

"I don't know. When I saw Special Police screaming orders and running all over the place, I got real scared. I ran and hid in Linen Closet. Please, sir, don't tell nobody. I didn't do nothing wrong."

"So you never saw a package?"

"No, sir. Never."

"You have my word. All of this is just between you and me. Do you know what happened to that package?"

Manny shook his head vigorously. "No, sir."

"Now this is important. Does anyone else know about it? Your brother, maybe?"

"Oh, no sir."

Trevor sighed deeply. "Thanks for tipping me off. I promise to help your brother to the extent I can. I'll draft a letter to the management, recommending that they bring your brother onto the staff here. Do we have a deal?"

"Yessir, thank you, sir," said Manny, smiling as a wave of relief washed over him.

"But one last thing, and this is important, Manny. You know what goes on at Deera Square here? 'Chop Chop Square'?"

"Yessir," said Manny quietly

"Then unless you want us both to end up there, you can never tell a soul – not even your brother about any of this. This is life or death, Manny. We could get beheaded and crucified over this. And your brother could rot to death in some filthy Saudi jail. And your family back in Manila would starve, begging in the streets. Understand?"

"Yessir, I do, sir," he said softly, terrified at the thought. Then he paused, searching for the right word. "Sir, what is going on? What are they looking for? The package?"

"Yes," Trevor said. "And anyone found with it will surely get beheaded in Chop Chop Square. Just knowing about it could bring an awful, agonizing death at the hands of Prince Mohammed."

The color drained from Manny's face upon hearing this.

"I tell nobody, sir." He vigorously shook his head. *"Nobody."*

ASPEN, COLORADO

Prince Bindar poured himself three shots of single malt whiskey over ice. Lagavulin, with its smoky, peaty taste, was his personal favorite, but he had fully stocked his bar with every high-end label. He went out onto his private wraparound deck to relax with his drink and enjoy the spectacular mountain vistas.

He always drank in private. As a nephew of the king, he was a defender of the faith in an Islamic theocracy, and therefore did not even let his servants and staff witness his imbibing. Most of the Saudi royals and wealthy commoners drank outside the Kingdom – and many did inside the Kingdom. Every royal surreptitiously kept a fully-stocked bar in his palace, under the guise of catering to western business visitors. He'd once visited the hottest nightclub in Cairo, Sultana's, and witnessed his countrymen guzzling champagne by the magnum, wolfing down hors d'oeuvres and chasing anything in a short, tight dress. This kind of behavior, he thought, undermined the authority of the royal family and courted disrespect.

It had cost him $125 million to build this mountainside palace of 56,000 square feet on ninety-seven acres, complete with an underground garage for sixty cars, a movie theatre, barbershop and beauty spa, indoor and outdoor pools, a 10,000-bottle wine cellar, and a permanent staff of twelve. It was a badge of honor for the Prince to host Jack Nicholson, Hunter S. Thompson, Ethel Kennedy and her brood and many other tabloid swells, along with the usual Wall Street and Washington grandees in his party gallery, which could accommodate 450 guests.

He had recently brushed off widely publicized charges by the British media, alleging that major European arms manufacturers had paid more than $3 billion into overseas bank accounts controlled by him. He surmised that stonewalling any such problem would cause it to eventually dry up and blow away. For if his father and uncles were not concerned about it, who on earth could call him to account, except Crown Prince Mohammed bin Salman? After all, they were doing much the same things in their own business dealings, and as long as everyone kept to his own turf and did not cross a more powerful member of the royal family – a "taller prince" – it was business as usual. Conflict of interest did not exist as a concept in Saudi.

Americans, he thought, *are foolishly naïve and fanciful about the workings of the real world out there. They'd actually attempted to legislate a kind of Yankee-Doodle morality with their silly Foreign Corrupt Practices Act, prohibiting overseas bribes in doing business. What a joke! All they had succeeded in doing was tying the hands of their big exporters, giving a major advantage to the Brits and French and Italians, who labored under no such strictures and were masters of " facilitation payments".* The Prince himself was under no illusions.

When Robert Perkins, the former Deputy Director and CIA Middle East Regional Station Chief, approached him in late 2010 about a top-secret undertaking in-Kingdom, the "Gemini Project," Bindar instantly recognized it as a major opening for him. If there was one thing the royal family feared, it was the Islamic and anti-royal terrorism in the region, and the threat it might pose to the Saudi regime. This was why Bindar and high-ranking royals kept back-channel access to the madrassas and the imams who ran them out in the western provinces, where Wahabism and jihad were the staples of their intellectual diet. As long as the royal family was surreptitiously funding their activities through off-shore "foundations" and other shadowy vehicles which masked true ownership and control, this tenuous arrangement worked. The religious extremists had accepted as an article of faith that as long as they pursued their goals outside Saudi, the government would not move on them. So far the arrangement had worked. But the events of 9/11 had left a bitter aftertaste with men like Perkins, who were determined to prevent such a recurrence – say, a dirty bomb detonated in the New York subway or the Washington Metro, or a jet drone delivering its fiery and lethal payload into a secure facility.

With Perkins's initiative, Bindar had eagerly seized upon this opportunity to raise his status in the royal family, to set himself head-and-shoulders above his cousins, to demonstrate to the family elders his foresight, wisdom and vision. At the insistence of Robert Perkins, he arranged to be the sole intermediary between Saudi Arabia and the Americans so that the king and his coterie of advisors would have plausible deniability. It was a classic "don't-ask-don't-tell" setup. He would share information only with the family elders, and only on a need-to-know basis. In sum, he would have sole and exclusive dominion over the project, which was what Perkins had demanded. Too much information in the wrong hands could jeopardize everything.

The missing money and diamonds in Kingdom were a pittance by the Prince's standards, but it did represent the continuing – and now, urgent - level of commitment by the Americans. But for him, it was a matter of "face" – respect. Whoever had the stolen wealth would eventually slip up, whereupon he would be immediately and brutally eliminated. So far on this project, over $2 billion had been funneled to the Prince, with even bigger sums to come. Out in the Empty Quarter, with the early completion of an airstrip capable of handling large commercial and heavy-cargo aircraft, the construction schedule had been accelerated and was in its final stages.

But he was troubled by the missing Project Completion Report. If it fell into the wrong hands, it would provoke a cataclysmic response. Bindar was no naif. He knew exactly where the pressure points, the sensitivities, could be found. If things went according to plan, it would ensure that he could achieve for himself what at one time seemed an impossible dream.

RIYADH

Souheir Fahad retreated to her inner-bedroom, her inviolable private sanctuary, and double-locked the door. How awful it was to feel so threatened and hemmed-in, deeply troubled, with nobody she could talk to and nowhere to turn. It was at dark moments such as this that her thoughts inevitably drifted to suicide. She had brought with her from New York an ample supply of sleeping pills – a quick, easy and painless way to escape all this.

All this, she thought, as she stripped nude and stood in front of her full-length mirror. She ran her hands along her curvaceous hips, at once admiring and then wishing they were fuller, cupping her ample breasts and light-brown nipples. Then very slowly and deliberately she slid her hands down her body, pressing them against her flat stomach and holding them there.

"This womb once held a child," she whispered. "A child that I desperately wanted to bear and love for eternity. Could I ever be forgiven for what I did? I *had* to do it – out of fear, a sense of family duty, out of the sheer shame that would come from having an out-of-wedlock child, an unthinkable offense under Sharia law and Saudi custom."

The father, a Jewish graduate student at NYU, would have only aggravated the matter had she disclosed that. The loss of her virginity was bad enough, a capital offense, but an abortion? Of a half-Jewish bastard child, a born infidel? She shuddered to think of the horrific ordeal awaiting her, torture followed by the executioner's huge, curved sword for the customary beheading. Then would come the crucifixion, a public display of the headless corpse on parallel bars, with the bloody severed head hanging next to the body in a see-through plastic bag. It was too gruesome to contemplate.

In the end, she had found herself the victim of an unforgivable betrayal: Her father had, without her knowledge or consent, arranged her marriage to an important business contact, where she would be the third and youngest of this man's wives. She imagined waiting hand-and-foot on these illiterate breeders, reduced to the status of a scullery maid, stuck with a man her father's age.

Why, oh why, did I ever come back? To get the family's blessing to pursue a career in New York? Yes, but there was another reason: I need their financial support to embark on my course. What a fool I was. What a gullible, fucking fool to have trusted them and their deceitful words. I cannot stall the premarital physical exam forever. It's been re-scheduled for the end of next week. And when they find I'm not a virgin, I'm a dead woman.

God, what will I do?

WASHINGTON, D.C.

Robert Perkins loved nothing more than being right. His old colleagues at Langley had a running joke about him: "Seldom wrong, but always certain." He sat alone in his office, reading the latest reports from the Kingdom regarding the broader details of the project. The sun was setting out over the Potomac, leaving streaky hues of pink and orange. He removed his glasses and rubbed his eyes, then leaned back in his chair and closed his eyes.

Ten years earlier, when he was formally introduced to Prince Bindar at a swanky New York cocktail party on the Upper East Side, Perkins had already conducted his own subreptive vetting and due-diligence process. He was convinced that the Prince was their likeliest candidate. With the sure patience of a seasoned hooker heating up a horny john over dollar beers in a corner joint, Perkins stealthily pursued him, mental checklist in hand.

For Perkins and his operatives had had their eyes open for a few years, on the lookout for the perfect Saudi collaborator. After the Prince had been identified as a likely choice, Perkins had done his homework on the man and knew just where this line of inquiry would go.

Who could conceivably oppose – or even question – a secret, state-of-the-art rendition center- in other words, a high-tech prison and torture facility - in the Empty Quarter of Saudi Arabia, deep in the desert, a project built and operated by Americans, where incarceration and "enhanced interrogation" could be undertaken without any oversight whatever? It was the perfect meeting of man and moment.

RIYADH

Trevor, dressed in the traditional Saudi gown, a white thobe with the red-checked keffiyeh headdress, asked the taxi driver to drop him on a dark side street behind the main soukh in the Old Quarter. It was a hot, crowded, seedy area, teeming with people of every ethnicity at all hours of night and day. Myriad pungent smells of spicy cuisines clashed in the fetid, smoky air, and the streetside charcoal grills served up tasty roast lamb and chicken rice plates. This was where most of the guest workers lived, in rundown rooming houses – Pakistani corrections staff, Korean construction workers, Filipino hotel staff, Indonesian waiters and manservants, African maintenance workers, with a sprinkling of oil jockeys from the American southwest, Great Britain and Australia. Most of the Asians and Africans shared squalid rooms and slept in shifts. Beefs and disputes were settled intramurally in this neighborhood; nobody ever went to the Saudi police, who themselves gave this area a wide berth for fear of physical danger. As long as nothing conspicuously dangerous or illegal was taking place, the area was left alone.

Fifteen minutes later, Trevor exited a taxi three blocks from his office building. Ten minutes after that, he was back at his apartment in the Al Khozama Hotel.

That coming weekend, Trevor planned to go into the office and catalog the serial numbers of the currency in the briefcase, in preparation for flight.

WASHINGTON, D.C.

Robert Perkins sat in the sunny, book-lined study of his Georgetown mansion, furiously leafing through his obligatory daily reading: *The New York Times, The Washington Post, The Wall Street Journal* and *Barrons.*

A warm wave of *schadenfreude* washed over him as he read of Crown Prince Mohammed bin Salman, and his connection to the brutal murder of *Washington Post* journalist Jamal Khahsoggi in Turkey.

What a ham-fisted buffoon, thought Perkins. *This guy is truly the gift that keeps on giving. A rank amateur who has no idea of what he's doing. We couldn't have scripted this better.*

On an impulse, he picked up his smartphone and punched in a number. It was a direct line to an operative in the Kingdom.

"Perkins here," he said. "What do you have on that person of interest, that Trevor Osborne fellow? Anything new?"

"Not really," came the reply. "He's been under close surveillance, and we think he knows he's being watched. We followed him halfway to Bahrain, and he apparently became aware of the tail on him. We alerted all of the checkpoints, so he and his car were thoroughly searched. Nothing. We've searched his apartment top to bottom, and scrubbed his office, which we also bugged, and we tapped his phone. Nothing. We also hid a GPS transmitter on his car. We haven't seen any extraordinary movement. This guy is either very cagey or simply the wrong target."

"Stay on top of him." ordered Perkins. "He's not a pro at this. If he's indeed our guy, he'll slip up. One wrong move and he's ours. Stay on him. Sooner or later he'll make a fatal mistake. And I do mean *fatal.*"

RIYADH

There had been no opportunity to retrieve and catalog the full contents of the briefcase. Trevor decided that he could not risk it until everyone else in the office was absent – and even then he had to be cautious.

He decided to wait until the upcoming Thursday, the beginning of the Saudi weekend, which was Thursday and Friday. The office would be closed all day, and he would arouse no suspicions. He frequently came to the office on Thursdays and Fridays to handle U.S.-sourced business.

It was just after noon on Wednesday, when the office was usually deserted until 4:30 for midday break. People left to have lunch, go home to nap, run errands. On a normal business day, they returned in late afternoon and worked until eight. Many chose to start the weekend early and did not return until Saturday. Trevor almost never left for midday break.

He assumed he was alone in the office until he heard quiet sobbing in the file room. When he warily tapped on the door, the sobbing abruptly stopped. He gently opened the door to see Souheir, sitting on a filing stool with her face in her hands. She looked up at him in surprise, her face wet, eyes swollen, sniveling, hair a mess.

"Oh, I'm so sorry," said Trevor, backing out of the file room.

"No, I am sorry, Mr. Osborne. I don't want to be seen like this. But please don't go."

"I have to. It's against the law for us to be even talking. You know that."

"Do you know that my father is spying on you for the Secret Police?" she demanded.

Shock stunned him, and fear slithered through his gut like an eel, and he felt a sudden sinking sensation. "What? Are you sure?"

"Yes. He tipped them off that you were going to Bahrain."

"How do you know this?

"I overheard him talking on the telephone. And I have a secret key to his confidential files. He knows nothing about it."

"Why are you telling me this?"

"Because we can help each other."

"How do you mean?"

"I need help. There is no one else I can turn to. And I can help you. I can tell you what is happening in secret here so you can protect yourself. Please."

"Are you in some kind of trouble, Souheir? And how can I help?"

"I should *never* have come back here after university," she said fiercely, "but I was forced to. I so wish I had stayed in New York," she sniffled. "I thought my family would understand. They don't."

"New York?"

"Yes. I attended university at NYU. I loved Greenwich Village, New York City, the freedom, the many wonderful things to do. I wanted to stay on and go to film school there. But my father forced me to come back here – where he betrayed me." Her voice dropped an octave with scorn. "He has arranged a marriage for me – to a man I don't even know. A man who is over sixty years old and already has two wives. Please help me get out of this country. I am desperate. I know what awaits me here, and I will kill myself first. You must help me."

"You know we're risking our lives to even talk. I will try to help you, but we must observe some strict ground rules. First, we cannot even *speak* if there is anyone else present. Nobody can ever know that we talk. Second, we can never meet in my office. We'll talk only in here, and only if we're alone in the office. And finally, no more of this suicide talk. Agreed?"

"Yes, and I thank you," she smiled through her tears and sniffling.

Now Trevor knew what the shouting match and crying in Fahad's office had been all about. He suspected something like this was transpiring. Souheir had already put them both in danger just by tipping him off. Was she setting him up? His intuition suggested otherwise. He felt himself being slowly but inexorably drawn into deeper water, losing control. But there was no way he would escape this hellish place without help. As frightening as it was, he needed her. He had to put himself into her hands. It was his only way out.

A light tug on a thread of memory brought back a vivid and frightening recollection to Trevor. He recalled the story of a Saudi princess who objected to being married off to a cousin her father's age. Princess Misha attempted to elope with her commoner boyfriend, whom she had met in college in Lebanon. They found a cleric who secretly married them. She then staged a fake death-by-drowning, leaving her clothes on a secluded beach in Jeddah, on the Red Sea. She had purchased a counterfeit passport, cut her hair and dressed in Saudi robes as a man. She was caught and revealed when Saudi security searched all of the passengers boarding a flight from Jeddah to Madrid. Her husband, booked on a different flight, was also caught. Both were arrested on a royal warrant. After a week of legal wrangling, both were sentenced to death and taken to the plaza in Jeddah. After begging for leniency for her husband, Princess Misha was killed by her grandfather – who ordered her blindfolded and shot in the face at point-blank range, with her young husband forced to witness it. He was then beheaded by one of her male relatives – not a professional executioner - with five agonizing strokes of the sword.

And this was a *princess.*

RIYADH

At mid-morning the next day, Trevor pulled into the underground garage at his office building. There was nobody in sight. He retrieved the briefcase from its hiding place, then went into his inner office and locked the door.

The cellophane-wrapped bricks of Euros were untouched, as were the diamonds. He unpacked the money, intending to note the sequence of serial numbers of the of the top bill in every stack. But he noticed, for the first time, an inner zipper-pocket in the briefcase. He opened it and removed a small envelope. Inside was an unmarked, red thumb-drive. He hurriedly re-packed the money and returned it to the hiding place in the ceiling.

After walking five blocks, checking over his shoulder to see if he was being followed, he hailed a taxi to the enormous new Hyatt Omnisphere, a place where he would not be noticed among the thousands of westerners in the weekend crowds, shopping in the mega-mall and using other services. He slipped downstairs to the hotel business center and rented a privacy booth for cash.

Then he locked the door, settled in, opened envelope and inserted the thumbdrive into his laptop.

Up came a large document. The cover page bore a legend in bold caps across the top: "THE GEMINI PROJECT- EYES ONLY – PROPRIETARY AND STRICTLY CONFIDENTIAL – NOT TO BE DUPLICATED WITHOUT THE EXPRESS WRITTEN PERMISSION OF VANGUARD INDUSTRIES, LTD."

Two hours later, Trevor lifted his head, feeling he had just aged about fifty years. His shortness of breath would not let him exit the first stages of shock. What he had read, and re-read, was simply unimaginable. Never in his life had he been so near to pure, unadulterated evil and greed. People surmised and conjectured about such doings, but it never was evidenced in any dispositive way – and certainly not in writing. But here it was. The last pieces of this puzzle finally clicked into place, and he now had the full picture.

"Fortune favors the bold," as his buddy Miles was fond of saying. But putting his pitiful ego into the path of this hideous juggernaut? He had already placed himself into the hands of a woman he did not know; what if she was unstable and flighty? What if she blurted out some secret – their secret – in another screaming match with her father?

What he held in his hands was unprecedented in its explosiveness, easily enough to blow everything else off the front pages of every major newspaper in the world. And he had the names of all the major players in this scheme, both in-Kingdom and out. All of the Americans were extremely wealthy and powerful, some well-known, most quite private. But one name was conspicuously absent among the few Saudis on this list: Crown Prince Mohammed bin Salman. And who the hell was this Prince Bindar bin Ahmed?

Trevor made a hard copy of the 250-page document and downloaded the contents to his new smartphone. Then he copied the contents onto another thumb drive, crushed the original under his heel and threw it into the trash before re-entering the mall traffic and melting into the crowd.

He now understood that he was in well over his head among such powerful and competing forces. There was only one thing to do: Call Miles Braxton and enlist his help.

LONDON

Prince Bindar looked out over the glowing orange sunset from his offices on the upper floors of an ultramodern Canary Wharf skyscraper. He smiled when he thought of this complex, the Americanization of the Old World, replete with a ground-floor mega-mall running the entire length of this cluster of tall buildings sitting atop the landfill of the old, decrepit East Docks.

Robert Perkins had left several messages in his private voicemail, so he decided to return those calls and be done with him for the moment. Prince Bindar already knew that they had run into a glitch in Riyadh, and that the cash and jewels intended for his people on the ground in-Kingdom had disappeared following the extreme stupidity of the American operatives. Bindar had used his backchannels in the Kingdom to put on the full-court press to find the loot, the sooner, the better. But of far greater significance to him and to Perkins was the top-secret project completion report, which had been one of the few communiques to identify the principal players in this effort.

Everything was now in jeopardy until that could be located and secured. He punched in Perkins's private line. It was answered on the third ring.

"Perkins here. Anything new in-Kingdom?"

"Not yet," replied Bindar. "This Osborne fellow may well be the wrong person-of-interest. Our people in Riyadh have kept a close watch on him, but he has done nothing out of the ordinary, and hasn't put a foot wrong."

"Can you have him arrested on some trumped-up charge and held until he talks?" asked Perkins.

"Yes, but that is too extreme at the moment, and bound to call attention to the project. Frankly, the available evidence does not point to anyone else.

But arrest and detention? Not just yet. But soon, if that package does not turn up within the next week. We may have to sweat it out of him. And we have very effective interrogation methods."

Perkins laughed shortly. "Yes, I know."

RIYADH

Cyber cafes, when grudgingly and finally permitted by Saudi officials, experienced an overnight growth spurt. They popped up in almost every section of the city, growing like weeds in the summer rain. They were frequented by young, hollow-eyed, sullen, unemployed, disaffected Saudi men, nearly all of them under the age of thirty, doubtless dreaming of jihad or a shiny new Lamborghini. The thousands of guest workers comprised the rest of the patrons. Down in the Old Quarter, there seemed to be one on every street corner. Many were twenty-four/seven operations, with the nonstop traffic of men remitting money home world-wide. But Trevor might stand out and be recognized in such places. So where could he go? To a Starbucks, of course. There were over a dozen in the central city, and all had free wifi. Westerners tended to gravitate to the familiar in unfamiliar circumstances, and this was no different.

Trevor went directly from the business center to the closest Starbucks which, as chance would have it, was about two-hundred yards away in the crowded, noisy mall.

He found a small table in the corner, staked it out, and went to get coffee and a pastry.

Then he carefully crafted an email to Miles Braxton, now a vice-president at Kroll Associates – the premier security and intelligence firm in the world.

It read: "Dear Miles: I'm still in the desert. I need a very important favor: some confidential background info on the attached list of individuals, with current contacts. Especially the Perkins guy. ASAP. This thing is HUGE. Please reply by email and give me a time, then I will phone you. Remember that pact we made years ago, in the back room of Bob the Chef's soul food joint, over draft beer and barbecued ribs? You could be a giant step closer to that Ferrari and much more, my brother!"

Enough of this frightened lurking in the shadows, like some timid prey animal. It was time to go on the offensive and seriously deal. What he had in his hands, finally, was real power – the power to save his own life and that of an earnest young woman, to disappear into a world of luxury and privilege - and the power to bring down or save the government of a wealthy sovereign nation.

If anybody could manage this nervy gambit, it was Miles.

RIYADH

Trevor's favorite elder back in Jamaica, his Uncle Winston, had a storehouse of tall tales from his days as a social worker in Chicago. "The world starts spinning at different times and different places for different people" was one of his favorite sayings.

For Trevor, the only child of cautious, hard-working Caribbean immigrants settled in Brooklyn, his world commenced its rotations with his meeting Miles Braxton. Miles, a child of Chicago's South Side in the Park Manor area, came from a long line of the hustling entrepreneurs for which Chicago was famous. His famous father, Herman Braxton, owned Braxton's Show Club, the premier South Side music venue and favorite of such popular stars as Nancy Wilson, Nat King Cole, Lou Rawls and Aretha Franklin. The old man had one hard line when it came to entertainment: No blues and no drugs – not even one joint. "That's not the clientele I want," he intoned. "Take that gutbucket shit over to the juke joints and dives in Englewood or Lawndale. I run a class establishment, where a fella and his lady can dress up and step out." He also built a motel for black travelers and a taxicab company that serviced the South Side – where white drivers would not go. His sidelines included operating an after-hours gambling joint offsite and fencing hot goods for the Chicago mob hijackers. Herman Braxton was instrumental in other areas of the criminal nether world as well, such a versatile fellow was he.

Miles had related a tale to Trevor, something that he'd learned as a youth from his father years earlier. If there was any moral in this scenario, it would have to be both cynical and profane. It was a quintessential "Tale of Chicago".

In 1962, Charles "Sonny" Liston, the top contender for the heavyweight boxing championship of the world, was denied a license to fight by forty-nine states and every U.S. Territory and Possession because of his criminal record, imprisonment and underworld connections. Not surprisingly, the sole exception was Illinois. This was because Herman Braxton had quickly recognized a golden opportunity and commenced backchannel negotiations with his cronies in Springfield to bring off the license for a championship fight in Chicago, pitching it as a boon for city business and prestige. The biggest stumbling block was that Liston was owned by Philadelphia mobsters Frankie Carbo and Blinky Palermo, whom he also served as a kneecap-breaker and general enforcer. Heavier artillery was needed. What to do? Braxton approached powerful Chicago mob kingpin Sam "Momo" Giancana to facilitate matters. Giancana had long sought an entry into the fight game, and here it was. He was thrilled at the prospect of controlling the most prestigious prize in all of sport: the Heavyweight Boxing Crown. The Philadelphia hoods had no appetite for dealing with a violent uber-thug like Giancana, mainly because of his history of treachery and sadism, but they had to cut him in on the deal to get the license. It was the only avenue into the ring for their man, and Giancana knew it. Then Mayor Richard J. Daley, for his cut, weighed in to endorse the fight, declaring "The people of Chicago believe in rehabilitation and second chances." They also believed in the richest prizefight in boxing history. Liston got a license to fight for the heavyweight championship of the world in Chicago's Comiskey Park, where he decimated Floyd Patterson in the first round, and everybody else went to the bank. Now the Philadelphia hoods were indebted to the feral Giancana, whose next move, predictably, was to muscle in on them and take ownership of champion Liston for himself. They knew better than to cross or deny a man like Giancana, a mob boss of the old school who murdered his way to the top. And for years later, Chicagoans would laugh and claim that "Boss Daley delivered The White House to Jack Kennedy, and Momo Giancana stocked the Presidential bedroom with hookers!"

For his part, Herman Braxton steered Liston to a realtor who sold him, for cash, a grossly overpriced twenty-one room mansion in a fancy neighborhood on the South Side, kicking back an exorbitant finder's fee from the transaction to Braxton. But Braxton was not without a beneficent side; he taught the illiterate Liston to proudly write his name in cursive so that he could avoid the humiliating "X" that he'd previously affixed to documents. Then he persuaded Liston to put that signature on an unrestricted general power-of-attorney, which Braxton used to clean out Liston's bank accounts and drop a jumbo mortgage on the mansion while sucking out the equity – thereby propelling the house into foreclosure, leaving Liston holding the bag. Braxton later bought the property at a rigged auction for pennies on the dollar.

The fleecing of the illiterate, painfully shy Liston, the 24th of 25 children of a violent and abusive Arkansas sharecropper, was full-on and would not be complete until they'd picked him clean. Eighteen months later, the flashing fists and quicksilver moves of brash young challenger Cassius Clay would permanently derail the Liston gravy train in a huge upset.

When Liston took his dive in their second fight, it was abundantly justified: he owned exactly 10% of himself, and his wife and stepchild had been kidnapped and were being held hostage by the Black Muslims in Chicago – the same people who'd gunned down Malcolm X in broad daylight before hundreds of people only two months earlier - as insurance for a victory by the newly-named Muhammad Ali. As Herman Braxton observed, "Yeah, Liston came in here going for bad. But those hard-headed ex-cons in the Nation of Islam scared the dogshit out of him. His mob bosses couldn't protect him or his family from them. So why should he stay in there and take a beating? They totally shot his ass through the grease!" When questioned about all this, Liston would only darkly mutter "Man, them Muslims crazy." Frankie Carbo and Blinky Palermo had slunk back to Philadelphia minus Liston, with their tails tucked

Chicago was a nightmarish ordeal for Liston and his handlers, but not atypical. Liston ran like a scalded cat for Las Vegas, his kind of town, where he was comped at every bar, and where he could indulge his simple tastes: blackjack, craps, whiskey, hookers, marijuana, cocaine and heroin. And where, six years later, penniless, he would be found dead of a heroin overdose.

It was scant wonder, then, that until he was about ten, Miles thought that every father left the house in the morning armed. This harsh, acquisitive world influenced him in myriad and strange ways. As his grandmother always said to him "You were old when you were young."

"Why do you think he told you about all that?" asked Trevor

"Well, at the time Pop was dying of cancer, and he said he'd always had a bad conscience about it, and that maybe he was just reaping the payback for the shit he'd done. Before that, whenever I asked, he'd just say 'I do the shit I do so you don't have to.'"

Miles continued. "But you know what my takeaway was? That outlaws and artists all know that the 'official story', the one they toss out there to pacify the morons, is *always* a motherfucking lie."

Just talking with Miles gave Trevor the much-needed comfort and support for what lay ahead. He felt relieved just having someone else in the know, and he turned over the planning and execution to Miles.

He slept soundly that night, knowing that he'd just gained the upper-hand.

RIYADH

The studio apartment in the Al Khozama Hotel felt like a jail cell to Trevor, and he wanted to switch to another hotel. But as much as he desired, he could not change his routine without arousing suspicion. And he desperately wanted to go someplace where he did not have to sleep with one eye open. So for now, he had to live and sleep under constant surveillance, uncomfortable as that was, under a giant, unblinking eye. He only went there now to shower and to sleep, difficult as that was. A good night's sleep was an impossible dream right about now. If he stayed where he was, he was a sitting duck for surveillance, detention, arrest or worse.

But he got a directive from Miles. Going to another hotel would only invite intensified scrutiny, so that was out. Getting a room down in the seedy Old Quarter was also a nonstarter, for obvious reasons. What to do? Find a room outside of Riyadh, but where? In an American compound, advised Miles.

Of course. American expats and their families lived outside of the major cities in walled communities with their own grocery stores, banks and other amenities, right down to Little League. These colonies, sitting smack in the middle of the desert, were like small pockets of Americana. Saudis were forbidden to enter these areas, and the religious police ignored them. Miles had checked the online listings and found the perfect one: A elderly American expat, an ARAMCO executive, and his wife were looking to lease an in-law apartment adjoining their house, preferably to a single western male. It had a separate entrance and the cost was reasonable. At least he would feel a little safer inside those walls. He phoned them, introduced himself, and asked to meet with them right away. They agreed.

Trevor had not forgotten about the GPS on his car, and he knew that any evidence of his visits to the American compound would send a red alert to whomever was shadowing him. He took a taxi to an Avis office in downtown Riyadh and paid cash for a month-long rental. He would find a public garage to stash the car so that it would remain a secret; he would drive it to and from the compound, and leave his own car in the hotel garage except for travel to and from the office.

When he arrived at the entrance gate later that afternoon, his name had already been supplied to security, so they waved him through. It was his first time ever inside one of these places, and he noted the faux Rockwellian touches in the nearly-identical tract houses, including the astroturf everywhere in lieu of real grass and remarkably realistic fake palm trees. The Jahoskys, a quiet, pleasant, elderly couple from Florida, were winding up their ARAMCO tour in Saudi and wanted a little more off-the-books income to take home with them. Trevor paid them in advance for six months, and, delighted, they immediately gave him a gate pass and codes for getting in and out. They were also enormously impressed with his being a lawyer in Saudi. He felt a twinge of guilt at coming into their lives bearing his awful burdens, and wondering whether they might be implicated in what he was doing. But if he maintained his place in the hotel, occasionally dropping in for mail and personal matters, while keeping his place in this community a complete secret, the secret police might track him to the colony, but no further without revealing themselves. Any more intrusive moves would be slowed, but ultimately not stopped.

———⁓⁓∘ᴄ∾⊱∘⊰∾ᴐ∘⁓⁓———

Things at the office were quiet and normal, so he took to spending most of his casual hours there or at one of the nearby Starbucks, where he could sit most evenings with his laptop and phone without being disturbed.

Souheir was also in the office most of the day, and she treated him exactly as she had before – like a piece of furniture, hardly ever looking his way. But she waited until midday break when everyone else was gone to wordlessly motion Trevor into the file room.

"You need to be aware of what is happening," she whispered. "I overheard my father last night in his office at home. He is meeting with the secret police next week. They plan to detain you for questioning after the meeting and hold you indefinitely. He never mentioned why. What do they want from you, Trevor? Why are they doing this to you?"

Fear and dread made him nauseated.

"I don't know," he lied feelingly, opening his eyes wide and extending his upturned palms and shrugging. "They think I had something to do with the bomb scare at the Al Khozama last month. I've already been interrogated by the police, and I swear I know nothing about that. I'm not a political animal at all. Are you sure about this?"

"I can only tell you what I heard firsthand. But what am *I* going to do? My wedding (and here she closed her eyes tightly and shook her head) takes place in three weeks. I must find a way out of here."

"Souheir, I'm working on a secret plan that would get both of us out of here. I can't tell you what is. But trust me. I'm looking out for you, too."

"Then you have to move quickly." She paused, struggling for the right words. "I must make a confession to you, Trevor." Here she closed her eyes again. "I am not – I am not a virgin. I had my first serious relationship in university in New York." Here her voice dropped to a tiny whisper. "I have never told anyone else. I have to go for the pre-wedding physical exam next week. I have postponed it as long as I can. When they find this out, I could be put to death."

The enormity of this confession moved her. Unexpectedly and on impulse, she hugged him – a strictly forbidden gesture – and kissed him on the cheek – aggravating it. Then she kissed him full on the lips – gently, but with a promise. He held her soft, lovely body closely, unable to quite let go. It had been *so* long.

Her fragrance and nearness immediately awakened a raging, hard erection, which he could not conceal. She sighed heavily, and he came to his senses, quickly backing away. Why invite yet another potential catastrophe in this accursed place?

"Um, let's not venture down this path – just yet," he said.

"Yes, I am sorry, Trevor. I will be more careful in the future. It's just that I have no one else to talk to, and I am so miserable and alone. I'm very frightened."

"Well, don't be scared. You're as bereft and alone as I am," he replied. "But caution is a necessity. One misstep and we both end up in Deera Square."

WASHINGTON, D.C.

Robert Perkins had spent a tiring day. Up at dawn to be driven to Annapolis to meet with old friends from the Company for a half-day's sail and lunch on the Chesapeake Bay, then back to Washington to put the finishing operational touches on The Gemini Project.

He was sitting in his Georgetown study, poring over recent reports, and allowing himself to half-believe that maybe, just maybe, that little problem in-Kingdom might simply evaporate.

Almost as if on cue, his personal mobile phone buzzed. He looked at the incoming number, which was unfamiliar to him and appeared to be coming from a wide-area satellite band, likely a disposable phone. He accepted the call.

"Good evening, Mr. Perkins," said the mature, buttery voice on the other end. "Am I in fact speaking with Mr. Perkins?"

"Yes," snapped Perkins, "who are you?"

"Let's just say that I know who you are, but you don't know me – yet."

It was Miles Braxton, plying his trade and relishing every moment.

"How did you get this number and just why are you calling me?" demanded Perkins impatiently.

"I'll get right to the point. You are, of course, familiar with The Gemini Project?"

Perkins felt his blood run cold. Here it was, right in his face, with everything on the line. For the first time in decades his tongue felt like a brick in his mouth. He could not respond.

"Hello? Mr. Perkins? Are you still there?"

"Yes," said Perkins quietly, his mind racing madly for an appropriate response, looking for ways to keep this caller on the line, yet fearing what was coming.

"Please check your personal email after this call. In it you will find the first, middle and last pages of your Gemini Project Completion Report. I have the whole document, of course. But it would truly be a shame if that report somehow got released to Crown Prince Mohammed bin Salman, now wouldn't it? And so close to fruition, too. What do you think he would pay for it? What do you think would happen if his personal attorneys in New York and London got their hands on it? You know, the big boys at Cravath Swaine on Wall Street and Clifford Chance in London? Can you imagine the jeopardy for all your people in the Kingdom? Can you visualize the bloody orgy of death in Deera Square?" Miles taunted.

"You fucking bastard," Perkins whispered fiercely into the phone. "Who are you and what do you want?"

"I want safe, private passage out of Saudi for my client and his fiancée. They both have valid passports. We want no questions asked, no searches, nothing. You can arrange that through Prince Bindar, your protégé. He will also know how to compensate her father after the fact."

"Prince Bindar? What the hell do you know about him?"

"In a word, everything. Listen, Mr. Perkins, we don't give a flying fuck what you and your billionaire friends do. We don't give a fiddler's fuck about Prince Bindar, Crown Prince Mohammed or that godforsaken pile of sand. It's really none of my business. I'm concerned about two people: my client and his fiancée. You transport them to Europe by military or chartered private jet and we will respect your confidentiality. You will never see or hear from me again. I won't say a word. And after Gemini is implemented, none of this will matter anyway. That's all I ask."

"I expect that you have the cash and diamonds?"

"What cash and diamonds? I don't know anything about that." Miles lied. "But what I *do* know is how Crown Prince Mohammed might react if he saw your Gemini Project Completion Report. And that's worth something. I'd say fifty million Euros, which is frankly nugatory under present circumstances. Time is of the essence, and I expect good faith. Which is why I want that amount immediately wired to and held in an account at a certain Caymans bank. The wire instructions are in the email. Once receipt of the wire is confirmed, you will arrange to transport my client and his fiancée to a destination in Europe to be determined. I will promptly turn over all tapes, drives, discs, electronic files, the works. And I'll instruct my office to destroy and certify destruction of all files. That's it, Mr. Perkins. I'd say your choice is fairly clear. Do we have an agreement?"

Perkins paused for a long moment, weighing the judiciousness of his words.

"If that's all there is, then I think we can make that happen. But how do we know we can trust you on this?" asked Perkins.

"Because, sir, you don't have a choice right now. And because I frankly don't give a shit about any of this. One way or another, I intend to get paid. And that money can come from you or MBS, I don't care. But understand that if my client stops checking in on a regular basis – to confirm and verify his safety – the Gemini Project report will be released to all those deemed appropriate – including all the major news services. When he confirms to me that the eagle has landed and they're safe and free, I am under express instructions to destroy all files relating to this."

"I see," said Perkins.

"Time is short. This must be done right away. Just between us boys, Mr. Perkins, I don't want them in-Kingdom when Gemini goes down. Today is Monday. I want them out of there no later than Friday night. Am I making things clear?"

"Yes," replied Perkins quietly. "But getting them out could be problematic."

"No, it wouldn't. I know all about the secret U.S. base outside Riyadh. One of your CIA Black Projects, if my sources are accurate. I believe that you were instrumental in the establishment of that facility. The Royal Saudi Air Force has a base right in downtown Riyadh. You can do whatever the fuck you want, Mr. Perkins. So don't try to bullshit me. I'll have my associate checking with the Caymans bank to confirm receipt. And once they're out of there, free and in the clear, you and I are done. They and I will simply vanish. Personally, I'd like to see your Project succeed. But this is business. Understood?"

After a long pause, he spoke. "All right," said Perkins. His voice conveyed defeat. It was new to him.

"I'll be contacting you again in a day or two to confirm details regarding departure. In the meantime, don't try anything foolish. It could get a lot of your people killed. And blow up a fuck-ton of your investors' money. For nothing."

Miles Braxton rang off and chuckled. His next call was to Trevor.

"Okay, bro, the kickoff went just fine. I'm sending you a recorded transcript of the conversation. Man, that old codger is so scared he doesn't know whether to *shit or go blind!*"

———

Robert Perkins was not accustomed to this. It was almost always *he* holding the whip-handle, the ace-up-the-sleeve, the tactical advantage, the old upper-hand. He was just exiting the first stages of shock at how such a simple error, a minor oversight, could possibly blow up the entire elaborate and painstakingly constructed plan. He needed to get to Prince Bindar immediately.

———

Perkins reflected on the glory days, when he and his friends in the CIA worked with virtually no oversight by any politician or body. Eisenhower had given them a blank check and turned his back. The onset of the Cold War had afforded them zero accountability – to *anyone*. Perkins worshipped the Dulles brothers: John Foster, the Secretary of State, and Allen, unquestioned head of the CIA, as secure in his fiefdom as J. Edgar Hoover. Winston Churchill famously said of John Foster Dulles: "He is a bull who carries his own china shop with him." And then there was Allen Dulles, the founding father of "regime change", who implemented his visions in dozens of countries around the globe, a reckless, unrestrained, gun-slinging bully, a man who rode roughshod over nations and people like a drunken, sporting lord. Perkins worshipped them enthusiastically and without reservation.

It was an unexpected stroke of upper-class *noblesse oblige* that Perkins should be befriended by George Herbert Walker Bush at Yale, where they both played on the varsity baseball team, and where Bush brought Perkins into his fraternity, DKE. But Perkins knew that he would never be tapped for any of the secret societies, let alone Skull & Bones – one of America's holiest inner sanctums. It remained a slight that made him feel ever more the upstart, the striver, the parvenu.

In the immediate aftermath of World War II, Perkins did what most of his friends did rather than look for employment. They drank. At 10:00 a.m. a half-dozen or so could already be found at the Men's Grill bar of the Yale Club in New York City – which was where Perkins was sitting when who should walk in but George H.W. Bush, himself fresh from the war. They renewed acquaintance, and then Bush invited Perkins to join him and his father – Senator Prescott Bush – for lunch in the main dining room with a friend of his father. That friend happened to be Allen Dulles, then Director of Central Intelligence. It was through this fortuitous connection that Perkins was hired by Allen Dulles.

Perkins sat at the chief's elbow, a young, impetuous aide-de-camp, all through the 1950s, making mental notes and giving his boss heart, hand and soul. Political assassinations, physical torture, disinformation campaigns, destabilization of nations, the toppling of uncooperative world leaders, and much, much worse was their stock-in-trade. But they saw themselves as the unquestionable stewards of America and its values, a bulwark against all foreign threats and dangers, known and unknown, protecting "vital interests".

Then it all came crashing down with John Fitzgerald Kennedy. Perkins despised Kennedy as a super-rich, over-privileged pretty boy, a premier narcissist and rabid womanizer, a man whose reckless appetites would surely put the country at risk. It was also clear that Kennedy was strong-willed, with a disturbing streak of independence. He was very unlike Eisenhower, who, in his assigned role of caretaker president, always looked the other way when it came to this crowd to give himself plausible deniability. With Ike, it was "Tell me only if there is an express need for me to know. Otherwise, stow it."

The inevitable collision, the crucible, came in April of 1961, with the Bay of Pigs invasion in Cuba, conceived, sponsored and funded by Allen Dulles, head of the CIA. Kennedy, newly-sworn into the presidency, had been kept in the dark until the last minute, then told that the mission depended largely upon air support, which only the president could authorize. Kennedy faced a serious dilemma in his young presidency: being forced into either a hasty, poorly-considered decision rendered under duress, or denying air support, playing it safe and taking the heat, which would eventually subside. He opted for the latter course, uncomfortable as it might have been; he was absolutely not gambling his nascent presidency on what he considered a hare-brained venture that would likely fail miserably.

The mission *was* a spectacularly dismal, humiliating failure, with nonstop finger-pointing, blame-placing and recriminations. Old Joe Kennedy, enraged, entered the fray. They weren't going to hang this one around Jack's neck. Seven months later, on November 28, 1961, President Kennedy presented Dulles with the National Security Medal in a formal ceremony at CIA headquarters at

Langley. The very next day, November 29, "Mr. Untouchable", Allen Dulles, long-time head of the CIA, was unceremoniously and without warning fired by Kennedy. He was physically and publicly escorted out of headquarters by three U.S. Marshals, making the humiliation complete.

Perkins, a disciple and true believer, was distraught. So were the minions of Dulles's loyal and fierce supporters within – and without – the Company. Dulles then opened a public relations and consultancy firm on K Street, where he worked in the shadows under private contracts for his former employer, remaining very much a player. Perkins was "Mr. Inside" to Dulles's "Mr. Outside."

It was in this context that Allen Dulles masterminded the assassination of President John F. Kennedy, with the aid and assistance of sympathetic insiders like Perkins. Why would they want the president killed? Because a mole with the Joint Chiefs of Staff had leaked information about Kennedy's plans for the future: To kick off his 1964 re-election campaign by announcing the unilateral, phased withdrawal of U.S. troops from Vietnam. For Dulles and his thugs, this was tantamount to surrender, the unraveling of all that they had worked for, and the end of the U.S. as we know it. They were taking no chances on this; Kennedy had to be stopped at all costs. And for Dulles, this would also be the sweetest revenge.

It was Perkins, by now the most trusted and loyal hatchet-man, who first identified and interviewed Lee Harvey Oswald, the perfect loser and stooge for his assigned role. Perkins, posing as a spy for Russia, instantly read Oswald.

For all his bravado and large talk, Perkins knew exactly who and what Oswald was: a spoiled, sissified, little mama's boy, a self-esteeming loser who'd shared a bed with his doting mother until he was twelve. He also shared his mother's delusions of his grandeur. The Russia business helped mightily, especially since Perkins had funneled the money for Oswald's trips to the Soviet Union to create a plausible paper trail.

When the final plan fell into place, Perkins and cohorts could not help laughing about the Oswald piece of the plan. With that mail-order, $19.95-foreign-piece-of-junk rifle, Oswald could not have hit the broad side of a warehouse at ten paces. There were two other concealed rifles – both Winchester 30.06 automatics with zoom scopes and silencers, both manned by expert marksmen - at the scene of that horror. Oswald was merely the cover, the pigeon who stood to take the fall. Jack Ruby, for a price, made sure that Oswald would never live to tell – or sell - his tale.

The crowning irony in all of this was the appointment of Allen Dulles to the Warren Commission. Perkins and the other insiders were amused and delighted at this turn of events, for it meant that the convoluted truth of the Kennedy Assassination would be forever buried.

Just as Perkins resolved to pursue and hound Trevor until he was cornered and killed for his impertinence. He would never live to tell *this* tale.

LONDON

Prince Bindar clicked off his phone call with Robert Perkins. Now he was worried about that problem in-Kingdom. Yes, his cousin, Crown Prince Mohammed, a psychopathic murderer, would react in the only way he knew: mass arrests and bloody executions in Deera Square and elsewhere. But as a primary concern, he knew that he had to protect his people on the ground at all costs.

A part of him yearned to speak directly with the mystery man in-Kingdom; while he generally trusted Perkins's assessments, he wanted to measure and gauge this person for himself. Too much was at stake. But events were now racing to their inevitable conclusion, and this problem had to be promptly resolved. Perkins, Prince Bindar and the Gemini Project sponsors were now fully exposed, and this simply could not be. It was an irritant, but a potentially major one. Bindar was rather like a high-stakes gambler who could not afford to look up from the table with such a big bank running. It was a nettlesome diversion from the real business at hand, and he wanted to wrap this up and move on to the closing of the principal effort with expedience.

He hated the notion of paying off an extortionist; it grated on him. Bindar wanted to personally convey that if there was a double-cross, the mystery man would be running for his life, looking over his shoulder for the rest of his days. He would be a dead-man-running, someone who could be tracked to the ends of the earth. But this was small-potatoes compared with the grand prize awaiting him and his cohorts on the Gemini Project, and besides, he consoled himself, it wasn't his money anyway. He texted Perkins: "Wire transfer approved. Will arrange transport on this end through RSAF. Let your friend know the consequences of breach of contract. HRH."

RIYADH

Trevor spent a restful Monday night in his cozy little apartment inside the American compound, occasionally awakening and wondering where he was. When his senses came to him, he rolled over and went back to sleep.

In his waking moments he thought of his next move with Perkins and his Gemini Project cohorts, wondering if he had missed some vital detail. Things would rapidly pick up speed in the next few days. Miles had arranged that Trevor and Souheir be flown to a private airstrip outside Amsterdam, and he would take it from there. They would hop an express train to an unannounced destination and quickly vanish into Europe and beyond.

Tuesday, during mid-day break, Souheir waited until they were alone in the office and motioned him into the file room.

"My father is going away on business on Friday afternoon, to Dubai," she whispered. "I have the combination to his office wall safe. I can go in and get both our passports tomorrow. He will be leaving from home. When he returns on Monday, he won't miss them right away. But this is more urgent now. If you get detained, both of us are dead."

"Listen," he whispered sternly, "be ready to go with nothing but the clothes on our backs. Understand? Stuff an abaya into your backpack, just in case. I'm taking nothing. Does your father suspect you? Does he think you might run?"

She shook her head.

"Say *nothing*," he ordered. "To *anybody*. This is a matter of life and death, Souheir. Understand? No good-byes, no departing words, *nothing*."

"Yes," she whispered, moving closer to him and looking deeply into his eyes. She closed her eyes and tilted her chin upward as his lips touched hers. They kissed lightly at first, and then more hungrily, and finally she thrust her tongue hard into his mouth. Their tongues entwined with passion, and they both began breathing deeply. He pulled away before losing control.

Trevor composed himself. "All right," he finally said. "Remember what I said."

"When I get the passports, I will leave them with you tomorrow for safekeeping."

"Fine. Be very careful."

WASHINGTON, D.C.

On Wednesday morning, Robert Perkins phoned Prince Bindar to confirm that the fifty million Euros had been wired to the Caymans account, and that receipt had been acknowledged. He inquired as to the exit plan for the two mystery people in-Kingdom.

"I am personally arranging it," said Bindar. "I'm having them flown to Amsterdam on a VIP military transport. There's no chance of recovering the fifty million Euros. That money will be wired on to an account in, say, Hong Kong, and then forwarded again to perhaps Panama or Singapore. That's where the trail will go cold. As for the cash and diamonds missing in-country, I'm guessing this fellow is in on that, too. And the evidence and circumstances don't point to anyone but one Trevor Osborne. I'm guessing it's him. But that's of no moment right now."

"I'd still be eager to sweat that guy with some very enhanced interrogation," said Perkins. "Fifteen minutes on a waterboard would just about do the trick."

"Under different circumstances, yes, I would agree," Bindar replied. "This is a minor distraction, one that needs to be quickly closed out. I hope you stressed to our friend that any thought of breaching our agreement will be signing his own death warrant. I mean that. I can reach out and get him anywhere in the world. *Anywhere.*"

"So can I. He understands. He knows all about my background, too. Essentially, this guy is a soldier-of-fortune. He will take the money and disappear into a life of quiet opulence. He's not interested in politics or crusades or complicating matters for us – especially if his hide is at stake. He knows better. This is a cynical fucking deal, but we have bigger fish to fry at the moment."

RIYADH

As the personnel began clearing out of the office early Wednesday afternoon for the Saudi weekend, Trevor and Souheir were again left in the office together. The moment they were alone, she motioned Trevor into the file room.

"My father has taken off the rest of the day. He leaves for Dubai on Friday and won't be back in here until Monday," she said, handing him a thick manila envelope. "I took these from his office safe just now."

"Our passports?"

"Yes."

"Good. We'll need them in Europe, you know."

"Trevor, what is going on? What will we do?" she whispered desperately.

"I've got a call tonight. I'll have more news tomorrow about leaving here. In the meantime, stay mum. Don't say or do anything out of the ordinary. We could go at any time now. Be ready."

"My father has this app, Absher, that allows men to track women under their guardianship. There's a special alarm that goes off if the woman enters any airport."

"No worries. We'll deal with that when the time is right. Just stay alert. Keep your eyes and ears open. Life and death."

"Yes, Trevor, I will."

"When does your father leave on Friday?"

"Around 5:00 p.m. He's dropping me here on the way to the airport."

"Good. I've created a document that might be helpful. It's a fake affidavit purportedly signed by your father, giving official permission for you to leave the country for educational pursuits in the U.S. They won't be asking for that here, but in Europe they might. It's a master forgery. I've gotten a fake consularization for better effect."

He reached into his pocket, withdrew a small box and handed it to her. "What is this?" she asked.

He smiled, breaking the tension. "It's an engagement ring," he said.

She blushed purple. "Is it real?"

"No, Souheir, it's a figment of your imagination," he teased. "Actually, it's a very good fake. A zirconium stone with a tin inlay. We may have to put on that act, you know. And take this, too," he said, handing her one of the disposable phones. "From now on you use this to contact me, but only if you have to. And stuff an abaya into your handbag. We might need it."

"When do you think we will leave?"

"Tentatively Friday evening, just after your father heads off to Dubai."

"Is there a chance he would see us at the airport?" she asked, alarmed.

"No. We're not going to any airport. I'll tell you where on Friday. Now listen carefully, here's the plan: You tell your father that you have work in the office on Friday afternoon. He can drop you there on his way to the airport, knowing that you'll be there alone. Tell him your brother will drive you home. I'll be waiting in my rental car downstairs, in the garage. It's a blue Subaru. The moment he leaves, we'll go in that car. Remember, no luggage of any kind. By the time anyone realizes we're gone, we'll be in Europe, free."

RIYADH

Trevor began feeling paranoid on Thursday, as the moment of truth approached. It was the Saudi weekend, with the business week commencing on Saturday.

He'd gone to the office early, when the place would be deserted, and collected important papers and other personal effects. In the file room, he grabbed a step-ladder and, after closing and locking the door, climbed atop it and pushed up the drop-ceiling tile in the far corner.

His briefcase was still there, untouched. He would collect it on Friday just before bolting. Then he returned to the American colony.

He sat in his little apartment, distilling his papers and effects down to those few things he would take with him.

This was a chess game, taut, tense and deadly serious. He had to stay two or three moves ahead of Perkins and Prince Bindar. That was why Miles had demanded that they be flown to Amsterdam. They would now be on the lookout for him in the huge Diamond District of Antwerp, having suspected him of that heist from the beginning. They would assume that this would likely be his first stop, to convert some of the gems to hard cash. And this is where he would fox them. As Miles Braxton was fond of saying: "Signal right, go left, and *floor* it!"

So let them go looking for him in Antwerp.

They would not find him there. Or anywhere else in this world.

LONDON

Prince Bindar made arrangements to be picked up at Canary Wharf by helicopter early Saturday morning and flown to Gatwick Airport, where he would board his private jet and make the one-hour flight to a private airstrip at Ypenberg, about thirty-five miles outside Amsterdam.

He would be on his way to meet the two travelers from Saudi Arabia. Something – he did not know what – impelled him to meet this man face-to-face. There was a quality of character, the sheer nerve, that made Trevor curious to him – if the malefactor, was, in fact Trevor. He wanted to look it in the eye, size it up, shake its hand – and warn it that one step out of line meant the rest of life on the run and a certain, grisly death.

He also wanted to impart a more urgent and personal message.

RIYADH

Trevor did not sleep a wink Thursday night. He felt a tight ball of tension in the middle of his chest, and a run of adrenaline fueled his barely controlled dread.

He spent the night rehearsing the plan for the next day and re-packing his important documents in a man-purse, laying out his clothes, moving around the little apartment with a nervous, hyperkinetic energy. He forced himself to think through alternate scenarios in case something went awry. There could be no slip-ups, no casual error, nothing. This was truly a matter of life and death.

Souheir sat silently at lunch at home on Friday with her mother, who chirped endlessly about the wedding reception plans: who would be invited, who would not be, and why, and so on in this vein. Her daughter barely heard a word she said, feigning interest, nodding at the appropriate times, and responding with monosyllabic answers.

Finally, her mother stopped abruptly. "Souheir, you are not happy with this. I can feel it."

Souheir feebly attempted a protest, but her mother waved it off.

"Listen, daughter, please listen. I know what you are feeling. *All* women feel this before they are wed. I felt it before I wed your father. But you must be strong enough to make your peace with the things we cannot change. Because we have no choice, my dear."

Souheir was now fully attentive and tuned in.

Her mother continued. "Let me tell you what my mother told me before mine: 'Find a tiny part of yourself and hold it close. Keep it all to yourself, nurture it, make it yours and yours only, and share it only with the people you truly love.'"

Souheir was repulsed by the very thought of a life lived in this manner, but she was determined not to let it show.

"I understand, mother," she said. "It is probably just nerves on my part. But it is so frightening, going into a totally new life," she lied feelingly. "I am strong. I'll be fine," she said, forcing a glossy smile.

"Everything will work out, daughter, God willing," she said. "Trust me."

———❧———

Trevor left the American compound at two in the afternoon, waved at the guards tending the gatehouse, and drove to his favorite Starbucks to have a bite and make some last-minute telephone calls on a disposable telephone. He'd eaten nothing in over twenty-four hours, and he had to force himself to choke down a veggie wrap with a Coke. His BMW remained parked in the garage of the Al Khozama so that he would arouse no suspicions. He called Miles to check in and update him, while Miles confirmed that the €50 million had hit the account and had been immediately forwarded to a bank in Panama, then on to Singapore with no trace left behind.

After lunch he drove over to his office building, parked in the underground garage, and checked to make sure no one saw him. Satisfied that he was alone, he rode the elevator up to the twentieth floor, entered the deserted office, and surveyed it one last time. Yes, he would be routinely shown on the security videos, but he would be long gone before anyone saw his image.

After checking his desk one last time, he turned off the light and slipped into the darkened file room. He stood on the footstool and pushed up the tile in the dropped ceiling. Yes, the briefcase with his swag was still there. He withdrew it, opened it, checked the contents, and immediately shut off the lights and headed back down to the garage. This operation took all of ten minutes. The briefcase was tossed into the trunk. He quickly donned a Saudi thobe robe and checkered headgear, the *keffiyeh*. He had just settled into the car to wait for Souheir in the cool, dark garage, when his private phone buzzed. It was Souheir. He clicked on.

"Trevor?" she whispered nervously.

"Yes. What's up?"

"Trevor, I am in the bathroom at home. I can't talk long. My father's trip to Dubai was cancelled. He's not leaving after all. I had asked him to drop me at the office on the way, so now he is coming to the office with me. He will discover our missing passports. What will we do?"

Trevor's stomach churned up bile. *Fuck,* he thought, as his mind raced madly for a solution. "Just act normal," he said slowly and soothingly. "I'm downstairs in the garage, in the car, waiting. Now listen up, here's what you do: After you get here, leave a file or some personal item in the car and go upstairs with him. As soon as you hit the offices, tell him you forgot it and need to go back down to fetch it. Put on your abaya in the ladies room. Get back down here and we'll leave immediately. I'm sitting in a blue Subaru. Okay? Better?"

"Yes," she said, relieved but still frightened by the enormity of what they were about to do.

"Good. Stay calm. Act relaxed. This will soon be over."

"Thank you," she whispered tensely, and clicked off.

When Souheir and Dr. Fahad pulled into the underground garage, there were only a few cars down there.

Trevor saw them as he slouched down in his driver's seat, watching from a darkened corner of that level.

When they arrived upstairs at the offices, the lights were out and the place was locked. Dr. Fahad stopped at his receptionist's desk to scan the mail before entering his office.

Souheir knew that this was it.

"Papa, I'll be using the ladies facility down the hall."

Souheir let the outer door close and then stepped into the waiting elevator, where she quickly put on her abaya and veil. After exiting on the garage level, she broke into a dead sprint toward the blue Subaru, the abaya flowing behind her. The car was already running and the rear door was standing open.

"Quickly!" she said as she slid into the car and closed the door. "He will discover it any second now!"

"Get down," ordered Trevor. "I need you out of sight!"

They drove up to the garage door, and Trevor reached for the door opener attached his visor. It was not there. Then, in a collapsing sensation, he realized that he'd left the opener in the BMW – which was in the hotel garage.

"Oh, FUCK!" he shouted. "I left the opener in the other car! We're locked in here!"

At that moment Souheir's phone buzzed. It was her father.

"Are you still in the lavatory, Souheir?" he asked.

"Yes, papa, I am so sorry, I just got my period so I'll be a little longer, okay?"

"All right." She rang off.

"There's gotta be an emergency exit here," said Trevor nervously. "Let's grab our things and find it!"

"Wait a minute," said Souheir. She ran to her father's car and found his opener. "Got it!" she called, "let's go!"

The car exited the garage into darkness. Trevor resolved to drive within the speed limit despite being totally wired. They reached the outskirts of Riyadh within fifteen minutes, and picked up the superhighway toward the King Khalid International Airport.

"We are going to the airport?" Souheir asked nervously.

"Not exactly," said Trevor. "We're just taking the scenic route."

Just then her phone vibrated.

"Trevor, it's my father again. What should I do?"

The phone continued to vibrate and buzz insistently.

"Ignore it. Make him call you back. He will. When he does, tell him you're in the emergency room at King Faisal Hospital, badly hurt, and to come at once. Make it sound good."

Sure enough, the phone began buzzing again.

"Okay now, do your bit," commanded Trevor.

Souheir took a deep breath and clicked on.

"Where are you, Souheir?" Dr. Fahad roared. "You were in my safe, you little bitch! Where are those passports? Where is my fucking money? Where the hell are you?"

"Papa, I'm in hospital! I've been attacked and badly hurt! I was stabbed and I'm bleeding!" she moaned. "I'm at King Faisal Hospital! Come at once, please, Papa!" Then she clicked off.

"That was good. Now turn off your phone," ordered Trevor.

"But he can still track me with his app," she protested.

"Then turn it off and throw it out the goddamned window," he ordered. "We're not going to the airport anyway."

She complied with this request, hurling the phone into the darkness.

Trevor exited the superhighway and turned back toward the city center.

"Where are we going?" Souheir demanded.

"Riyadh Air Base, nearer the downtown area," he said. "It's operated by the Royal Saudi Air Force. His app can't track you there. He'll be notifying authorities to swoop down on King Khalid International Airport. Except you won't be there."

As they neared the busy city center, they heard sirens screaming in the distance. Trevor could not immediately gauge their source, and suddenly felt nervous nausea. He instinctively slowed to below the speed limit, hearing the sirens grow closer.

"What is it?" asked Souheir sharply.

"I don't know," he replied. "I can't tell where they're coming from. Just stay calm."

The sirens were now very close.

Suddenly, two police cars entered an intersection from the left, just in front of them, pulled sharp right turns, and pulled up next to them, lights flashing. Trevor felt a sinking sensation until Souheir snapped "Be quiet. Let me do all the talking. If they ask you anything, just point to your throat and say nothing," she ordered.

The officer in charge came up to the door and shined a flashlight in Trevor's face, then to Souheir, who was veiled. She immediately began talking urgently and rapidly to him in Arabic, explaining something. He listened impassively as she spoke. The officer exchanged words with her, seeming to take a gentler tack. His flashlight turned to Trevor's face. He asked a question in Arabic, and Trevor shrugged helplessly and pointed to his throat while Souheir spoke up. The officer deliberately studied Trevor's face for several agonizing moments, while Trevor held his breath out of sheer terror. Rivulets of cold sweat dripped down his back as the officer stared intently, making up his own mind. Souheir suddenly moaned loudly, and cried out in agony. The light shifted back to her. Finally, he stepped back and waved them on with his flashlight as he turned and walked back to his cruiser. Trevor felt a tidal wave of relief wash over him.

"What was that about?" he asked, as he cautiously pulled away from the curb.

"He said they were looking for an American man and a Saudi woman. I guess they assumed you'd be white. I told them that I am pregnant and about to deliver, that my water had broken and we were on our way to hospital. I said that you are my cousin, and you cannot talk because of throat surgery. It worked, thank Allah."

———⟋⟍∘◌⟋◌⟍◌⟋◌⟍∘◌⟍⟋———

When they pulled up at the entry checkpoint for the Air Base, Trevor produced their passports, was waved through and ordered to park the car. They were escorted from the car into an office and asked again for their passports, which they produced.

"Is anyone else traveling with you?" asked the officer.

"No," Trevor replied.

"Please sign the manifest, both of you. What is your destination?"

"Amsterdam," said Trevor.

"Are you transporting any dangerous or illegal substances?"

"Absolutely not," replied Trevor.

He turned to Souheir. "And you?"

"No, sir," she said quietly.

"Are you both leaving of your own free will and volition?"

"Yes," they replied in unison, prompting a slight smile from him.

"I see. When you arrive near Amsterdam, you will be picked up outside the city and driven the thirty miles to city center."

"All right. When can we leave?" asked Trevor, impatiently.

"Whenever you are ready, it's wheels-up and you depart."

"Let me put it another way: How *soon* can we leave?"

"You're free to go right now."

"Then let's get underway," said Trevor decisively, looking at Souheir, holding his breath in disbelief that this was really happening. Now that he was so close to his goal – escape – he was impelled to go before anything could go wrong.

They were escorted out into the darkness and onto the tarmac, where the smell of jet fuel was strong. Awaiting them was the aircraft, a small, unmarked military transport, a Gulfstream V. The interior smelled like that of a new car. The captain was an American flight instructor, big and bluff and ruddy from the desert sun, and his co-pilot and assistant was a young Saudi officer.

"I'm Cap'n Jack Heflin. How y'all doin' this evenin'?" he asked, smiling and welcoming them aboard. He introduced his co-pilot, Amir, who doubled as the steward for the flight. Amir showed them the sandwich platter and soft drinks in the mini-fridge, and asked that they signal him if they needed anything.

"Now if y'all are ready to go, we're outta here. We'll be goin' nonstop to Amsterdam. We'll be cruisin' at 40,000 feet at a speed of 650 miles per hour. Total flight time should be about nine hours, maybe shorter 'cause we've got a light load tonight. Y'all should be in Amsterdam in time for breakfast and a maybe a visit to the friendly neighborhood coffee shop (here he winked knowingly). Amir will come back and open the liquor cabinet once we clear Saudi airspace. Buckle in, folks."

As the aircraft taxied to a takeoff runway, Trevor spontaneously took Souheir's hand in his, and closed his eyes, praying silently to a God he did not yet fully believe in. Souheir closed her eyes and prayed to Allah for mercy and deliverance.

The plane started its acceleration for take-off, rapidly gathering speed, smoothly lifting off and banking toward the Red Sea in the west.

Trevor looked down at the mass of twinkling lights below them as they climbed out of Riyadh. He squeezed Souheir's hand. Both of them were starting to dare to believe that this was really happening.

He turned off the cabin lights and snuggled up to her under a blanket. She responded immediately, burying her face in his shoulder.

Ninety minutes later, Amir's voice came over the intercom. "Good evening. Would either of you care for a drink? We just cleared Saudi airspace."

Both of them were still wide-awake – and still wired.

Trevor finally exhaled loudly, more a huge sigh of relief. "Make mine a quadruple scotch on the rocks!" he exclaimed.

Amir entered the cabin, switched on the dim cabin lights and unlocked the bar.

Souheir looked down into the inky darkness. "Is that the Red Sea down there?" she asked.

"Indeed it is, ma'am," replied Amir.

"Good. I will have a martini, straight-up."

Trevor refused to allow himself to believe. He would wait until he stepped onto Dutch soil, a free man. He had harbored a tiny, nagging doubt that the aircraft might at any moment be intercepted by Saudi fighter jets, turned around and forced to land. That worry slowly drifted away as they soared past Cairo and over the Mediterranean at 40,000 feet. But he still could not fully relax. It seemed that whenever he had one problem solved, two new ones would pop up to take its place in his catalog of worries. Getting out of the Kingdom was a major hurdle, the most immediate and daunting of his challenges. In the process, he had crossed one of the most dangerous and vengeful men on the planet: Robert Perkins. And he knew that even if he did try his damnedest to disappear, Perkins would scour the planet and eventually find him. He could run to the ends of the earth, and Perkins would not rest until he was tracked down and savagely murdered. That was simply the nature of such men. *All* scores had to be settled. They were not accustomed to being bested at anything, and it was *all* personal to them. And the problem was aggravated by one suddenly-glaring fact: Perkins would eventually locate his father. And Trevor wanted him protected at all costs. What once had seemed so simple had evolved into heightened challenges and steeper risks, rather like trying to catch a blizzard in a teacup.

When he first reached out to Miles, he had posed the question of disappearing. Miles was a crack skip-tracer and information miner – talents which were quite useful in his chosen line of work. He assured Trevor that there are indeed myriad ways of disappearing like a wisp of smoke, leaving no trace behind. One such way, Miles texted him, was awaiting Trevor at the American Express office in Central Amsterdam.

After the celebratory drinks, both Trevor and Souheir, emotionally and physically drained, darkened the cabin lights and slipped quickly into a sleep free of dreams.

YPENBERG, THE NETHERLANDS

Prince Bindar's private Global Express landed smoothly on the Ypenberg airstrip, outside Amsterdam. It was shortly after 9:00 a.m. on Saturday morning.

Ypenberg had been a vital airbase for first the Germans and then the Allied forces during World War II, serving as a refueling facility for Allied aircraft on their way to and from Germany and Italy. The base was finally closed in 2010 and sold to a U.K. firm, who used it for private aircraft and charters.

There was only a small stone cottage at the heavily fortified gate. The twelve-foot cyclone fencing surrounding the airbase was topped by rolls of electrified razor-wire. All manner of dire warning signs were displayed around the perimeter. A black SUV was parked inside the gate, idling.

Prince Bindar settled into the small conference room in the cottage and waited for the two arrivals from Saudi Arabia. His personal assistant notified him that the incoming flight was on final approach and would land shortly. He nodded and continued doing business with his smart phone. The assistant laid out coffee, tea and pastries on the conference room credenza.

Twenty minutes later, Trevor and Souheir were ushered into the conference room, where Prince Bindar stood to greet them.

"Mr. Osborne, I presume?" he said, smiling and extending his hand to Trevor

"Yes," replied Trevor nervously. "And this is my fiancée, Souheir bin Fahad. We have a letter of permission from her father."

Prince Bindar airily dismissed this with a wave of his hand. "I don't care about that, it is personal business between the two of you. Please be seated."

They all sat while coffee and tea were served. The Prince charmed them with his knowledge of American culture and life, sharing political and show business gossip, trashing President Trump as "a shockingly ignorant, oafish man-child" and "the worst America has to offer".

Trevor relaxed and actually began to enjoy this interlude with a Saudi prince.

Abruptly he looked at Souheir and addressed her for the first time. "May we please have this room? Mr. Osborne and I must discuss private matters. We won't be long, so you may prefer to wait outside in the hired car."

Souheir nodded shyly and left the room. Trevor was affecting an ease he was far from feeling; something ominous seemed to drift into the air.

"I know your history and background, Mr. Osborne, and I see that you are a very smart man. Yes, you know all about the Gemini Project, and it must appear transcendently evil. But evil is a relative concept, of course. And there is something afoot that you do not know. So let me take the time to explain it to you."

Twenty minutes later, Trevor sat open-mouthed with shock, staring blankly at Prince Bindar.

When he had collected himself, he spoke. "I-I don't know what to say. But I have one concern that supersedes everything." Now he looked the Prince directly in the eye. "I want you to call off the dogs. You must know who I'm talking about: Robert Perkins. I don't want to spend the rest of my life on the run, looking over my shoulder. And I especially don't want my father approached in any way. I would like you to guarantee our safety from Perkins. And as a show of my good faith, I believe this is yours."

He put his briefcase on the table, opened it, and pushed it across to Prince Bindar.

Very little could surprise Prince Bindar at this stage, but this gesture stunned him. He stared hard across the table at Trevor, actually seeing him for the first time, then he regarded the cash and gems.

"I'd like to buy your protection from Perkins, for both me and my father," Trevor said. "This is my good-faith purchase. I will keep my word to you. I don't want to be a hero. And I don't need or want anyone shadowing me around the world, disturbing my peace. Your highness, the only way Perkins will drop this is if he thinks I'm dead. You can tell him that I've been neutralized, eliminated, whatever you want to call it, that I'm out of the way for good."

Prince Bindar seemed to consider this. "You will need a new identity," he said.

"I already have one," Trevor replied. "I just want to be left alone. And I especially want my father left alone."

"Consider it done," replied Prince Bindar.

Then Prince Bindar closed the briefcase and pushed it back across the table to Trevor. "Keep it," he said. "I don't need it. You will. You must disappear for a year or two. After the launch of the Gemini Project, none of this will matter anyway."

Prince Bindar rose, indicating that this meeting was over. He extended his hand to Trevor.

"All the best to you," he said.

Trevor joined Souheir in the passenger seat of the gleaming black SUV, and they departed for Amsterdam.

AMSTERDAM

"Well, what are your plans?" asked Trevor, as the SUV sped through the flat, green countryside toward the City Center.

"I'm not sure," replied Souheir. "Everything happened so quickly, I could only think of escaping. I intend to return to New York City as soon as I can. But I might have a problem."

"How do you mean?"

"My father will have my passport invalidated and revoked so that I cannot travel. What will I do then, Trevor? I must get to America as soon as possible."

"You could apply for asylum, but from my scant knowledge of it, you will have to wait months for a ruling. But my friend will help you."

"How can he help?"

"He's getting us new passports. From Aruba. You can get a whole new identity."

"I cannot relax until I reach America. I know I will be safe there. I can't be snatched off the street and forcibly taken back. Like some other girls I have heard about."

"We'll email a photo of you to my friend. He can take it from there. Souheir bin Fahad is shortly going to disappear. What name would you like? Have you thought about it?"

She wrote it on a slip of paper, and, smiling, passed it to him.

"You've gotta be kidding me!" he exclaimed, laughing.

"Never more serious," she replied.

They were dropped at the Central Railway Station in the heart of Amsterdam. Both were wearing the only clothing to make the trip: Trevor in a blue-blazer with jeans, and Souheir in sweater and slacks. She had thrown her abaya into a trash-bin, telling Trevor "I will never wear one of those again. That part of my life is over for good."

The American Express office on the Leidseplain was crowded and busy of a Saturday morning. Trevor stood patiently in line as other customers – mainly Americans – complained of lost AMEX cards, cancelled reservations and similar problems. Trevor was merely picking up a package.

The DHL Courier package he expected had arrived. He produced his passport at the desk, took the package and immediately left without opening it.

———ᴡᴏᴏᴄᴏᴏᴄᴏᴏᴄᴏᴏ———

They picked up sandwiches and beer as they boarded the late-morning Trans Europe Express to Zurich. From there they would go to Paris and fly out. As they settled into the comfortable first-class compartment, Trevor began opening his package. He unfolded a handwritten note. It was from Miles. It read: "Lively up yourself, mon!" Trevor smiled as he slit open the heavy manila envelope bearing the official seal of the Passport and Citizenship Agency of Aruba. He extracted the handsome maroon passport of Aruba, and opened it to the photo page of his new identity: Eric Porterfield of Oranjestad, along with his picture. He showed it to Souheir.

"What do you think of it?" he asked.

She took it gingerly, almost as if it might disintegrate in her hands. "Is this real?"

"Yes. My friend has major connections in Aruba. This passport is official. It cost me $100,000 because I got it on short notice. He's getting you one, too. That should take the pressure off you."

"But Trevor, I don't have that kind of money," she protested. "My father had €30,000 in cash in his safe. I took all of it. That money and these clothes are all that I have in this world. I've got to start making some definite plans."

"Souheir, money will not be your problem in the very near future. I've paid for your passport, and when we get to Paris, you'll have the funds to open an account in your new name."

"What? How do you mean?"

"I mean that I made a deal with Prince Bindar. That deal made me very, very rich. I want to share some with you. I could never have gotten out without your help. I owe you."

"What kind of deal did you make with him?"

"You don't want to know. But you'll find out soon enough. Wait for it."

"Why are you carrying that briefcase so tightly?"

"Because I'm carrying everything *I* own in it."

The nine-hour train ride to Zurich got them there in the early evening. They talked and slept in the first-class compartment. Trevor finally asked Souheir something that provoked his curiosity.

"Souheir, why in the world did you come back to Saudi from the States? What were you thinking?"

She was silent and pensive for a moment. "Well, I never thought I could suppress all my feelings and go back to being a traditional Saudi wife. My father promised me that the choice of a husband would be mine, and mine alone. That way I could avoid an arranged marriage to some hideous, nasty old man."

"And he reneged on his promise the moment you got back, right?"

"Yes, he did."

"I heard the two of you one night in his office, behind closed doors," he said. "I had begun to guess it was something like that."

She paused for a long moment. "It was more dangerous for me than you know," she said quietly.

"How so?"

"Because…" she hesitated. "Trevor, please don't hate me. I-I had an abortion in New York. The doctors would have seen the telltale scar tissue. Please don't hate me," she pleaded."

"Hate you?" he repeated. "Why would I hate you for something like that? It was before you even knew me, and it doesn't matter anyway."

"I want to be totally honest with you."

"Well. Let me be totally honest with you. Early in the marriage, my wife and I were drinking, got careless and she accidentally got pregnant. The timing couldn't have been worse. We both agreed to her abortion because of a dozen other factors. We both suffered the guilt."

Trevor shrugged, "You did what you had to do. It's over and done. And I don't give a damn about it. I'm being totally honest. Read my lips: I. Don't. Care." She impulsively embraced him, and he impulsively kissed her.

A luxury suite had been reserved by Miles in Trevor's name at the famous Dolder Grand Hotel, which sat regally on a high bluff overlooking the city, reachable only by funicular from the business district.

They checked in and were ushered to their suite, which could only be described as "grand". Waiting for them in the suite were new clothes, toiletries and luggage. Also awaiting them was a large basket of fruit and a chilled bottle of Dom Perignon – all arranged by Miles.

The first thing Trevor did was strip in the bathroom, take a hot, soapy shower, and wrap himself in the heavy Turkish hotel bathrobe. When he emerged, he saw Souheir standing before a huge window, looking out over the lights of the city below. She turned to face him.

"I still cannot believe that not twenty-four hours ago, we were in that accursed place and our lives were in danger. If I'm dreaming, I don't ever want to wake up," she said, laughing softly.

"Bathroom's all yours," he said.

She came toward him and encircled him with her arms, hugging him warmly. Then she looked him squarely in the eyes for moment, then closed hers slowly as she raised her lips to meet his. First lightly, then firmly, then with total abandon as their tongues entwined hungrily. She abruptly pulled away.

"Let me get cleaned up first, then we can continue," she said saucily, winking her promise at him.

Twenty minutes later, she exited the bathroom, wrapped in the other heavy Turkish robe.

"Shall we celebrate with some champagne? I would love that," she said.

They moved out onto the terrace overlooking the city and into the chill night air, where they drank the entire bottle. Finally relaxed, they opened another and commenced laughing and joking about their escape, their feelings, fears and hopes.

"Trevor, if you don't mind my asking, why is a guy like you divorced?"

"I married somebody who had no loyalty to me. To her, I was just another business deal. When I failed to measure up to her expectations, she dumped me and found someone more suited to her. She did me a huge favor."

"Do you miss her?"

"How can you miss someone who was never fully committed to you, who was so selfish as to be emotionally unavailable? She never gave a shit about me. Do I miss her? It'd be like missing a toothache. No, not at all."

"Methinks thou dost protest too much," she quipped, her dark eyes dancing with mischief.

"No, seriously," he said. "I just know my own mind and what happened to me and why. I don't hold grudges; I just remember facts." Then shifting gears, he said, "I'm gonna go pull out the sofa. We've only got one king bed in here."

"Why do we need the sofa?" she asked. "You should be comfortable, too. I don't mind that we sleep in the same bed. Do you?"

Surprised by so frontal an approach, Trevor quickly responded "No."

"Okay," she said. "But first let me answer a question you asked. You needed to know what my new name would be. I gave it a great deal of thought, and decided on a good American name.

"'Aretha Turner'? You're sure? The Queen of Soul and Tina Turner? Really?"

Souheir beamed. "I was never more serious. Tina is a Swiss citizen and lives here in Zurich now, so it is a paean to her."

"I like it," he said. "Miles certainly did. He thought it was a gas!"

"I'll turn down the bed. Just go into the bathroom for two minutes, please."

When he returned, the room was pitch black.

"Come and join me, Trevor," she purred. "Leave the robe on the chair."

He slid naked between the silken sheets, suddenly very shy about the circumstances. He simply did not know how to approach her. So he reached out his hand to her, lightly touching her shoulder. She pressed hard against him, and a passion he could not believe burst from this quiet, dark-haired beauty.

"Thank you, Souheir. You saved my life."

"And you saved mine," she whispered.

He hugged her, ran his hands through her long, lustrous black hair, kissed her neck. She shifted to face him in the darkness, finding his lips and lightly kissing him, then thrusting her tongue hard into his mouth, as if trying to thrust it down his throat. He ran his hands over her soft, full buttocks, stroking her body while exploring her mouth with his insistent tongue. Then he took her free hand and placed it on his rock-hard penis, encouraging her to stroke him – which she enthusiastically performed. His hand stroked her smooth thighs, and then came the moment of truth: he slid his hand down between her closed thighs, which she initially resisted, clamping her thighs tighter. Then, slowly, she opened them and let him stroke her wet vulva, as lubricant began dripping from his thick, engorged penis. They kissed deeply as each massaged the other.

"I want you inside me," she moaned. "Please," she begged with tears in her eyes, "I need you now. Please, put it in!"

She opened her thighs wide for him, her vulva lips all sugar-and-glue, swollen and puffed open, her clitoris standing up, red, wet and erect.

He entered her slowly and gently as they both moaned softly.

"Fuck me hard," she whispered. "I need it badly."

"Baby, I'm gonna knock the bottom outta your sweet pussy," he whispered feverishly. "I'm gonna shoot all my sperm deep in your belly. I'm giving you enough seed to make a million little brown babies!"

Souheir giggled. "I'm gonna milk every drop of sperm from your balls! Give me all your baby-batter! Come in me, sweetie! Gimme that nut! Shoot it deep in my wet, naked pussy!"

The torrent of dirty talk was pure aphrodisiac for both of them.

And away they went, humping and rutting into the Swiss night. They had sex three times that night, again at dawn, and once more before they arose at noon.

It being a Sunday, they decided on a lazy day inside their luxury suite, ordering room service, reading, watching television. The banks would not be open until the next day, so there was no urgency about anything. They never left the suite. Nothing had to happen today.

That night, they were hard at it again, making the sweet music of the bedspring symphony.

WASHINGTON, D.C.

Robert Perkins read and re-read the email from a field representative.

"Subject traveled by train with an unknown female companion and was followed from Amsterdam to Zurich, where they registered at the Dolder Grand Hotel. Train stations and airports are under surveillance to record his next move."

Perkins thought, *Yes, that's right, keep that sonofabitch in your line of vision at all times until the right moment presents itself. The impertinence of that young, black bastard!*

He won't live to enjoy that fucking money he stole. Not if I can help it.

ZURICH

Trevor awoke early Monday morning, alert and filled with a nervous energy. The strenuous nights after their arrival left them totally spent, but a catharsis, a relief from the tension of a terrifying flight to freedom, was in order. But he was fully recovered and in control of his senses now.

Miles had warned him that they would likely be tailed and shadowed once they got to Europe, so he had arranged with an executive long-distance limo service for them to be picked up in the service garage attached in the rear of the Dolder Grand, which was reached by a winding, mountain road rather than the fancy funicular. No one would see them leave.

Trevor wasn't certain if he was paranoid, or if there really was someone just beyond his peripheral vision, someone out there in the shadows, someone watching his every move, and his instincts rarely played him false. He could just *sense* a malevolent presence behind him. He would be carrying a fortune in a briefcase, in public, as he opened accounts under his new name, Eric Porterfield, citizen of Aruba. His first task would take him to the Diamond District, since the bulk of his fortune was in diamonds. His hope was to convert most of the gems to bank checks and letters of credit, valid anywhere in the world. He was carrying too much cash, and most of this would find its way into safe deposit boxes under the flashy Bahnstrasse, whose street is literally paved with gold. The security of a black SUV with darkened windows was better suited to this occasion, along with the highly visible, heavily armed Swiss National Guard patrolling these areas. Whoever it was – if, in fact, there actually was somebody tailing him – would be looking for him at the airports and train stations once they realized he had given them the slip.

And then there was Souheir – or, as she preferred, "Aretha Turner" – and her course. Miles had ordered an Aruban passport for her, and Trevor would

118

make certain that she reached the U.S. safely with two million Euros in cash, and then *adios.*

But Saturday night had altered his thinking. Did she do it out of simple gratitude, or was this the beginning of something? She had not mentioned anything about her plans for life after, except that she was returning to the West Village of New York City. At the moment she showed no inclination to leave, but perhaps it was just a measure of how much she needed him now. She was welcome to stay with him for as long as she needed.

Souheir suddenly interrupted his reverie. Her groggy voice asked "What time is it, Trevor?"

"You awake finally?" he asked pleasantly. "It's 7:30 a.m. We need to get packed up and outta here. We're going to be picked up in the out back. I've ordered coffee, tea, juice and pastries. I already checked out online. Pickup time is 9:00." He tossed her robe to her as she sat up in bed, shaking out her long hair.

She smiled at him as she wrapped herself in the robe and clambered out of bed. Then she impulsively embraced him. He responded in kind, stroking her hair and holding her close.

"I'll be ready in half an hour," she said, breaking away and entering the master bath and closing the door.

No one observed them when they used the service elevator to go down to the basement level, through which they left the hotel via the underground service garage in the back, both wearing dark glasses and baseball caps pulled down around their eyes, and quickly entered the waiting SUV with blackout windows.

———∿∿∘⌒∘⌒⌒∘⌒∘∘∿∿———

Souheir read fashion magazines and waited in the SUV for Trevor to finish his business, first in the Diamond District, near the Bellevue-Niederdorf area, then at the Union Bank of Switzerland on the Bahnstrasse.

When he returned to the limo at noon, he felt some sense of accomplishment: bank drafts and letters of credit totaling €42,000,000 for half of the twenty diamonds he possessed and most of the cash, with the remainder of the diamonds stashed in the safe deposit box at Union Bank. Then there was the money in The Caymans, which Miles had wired first to Panama and then on to Singapore. But the nagging worry, the stone in his shoe, was the danger to which he had exposed his father. Somehow, he had to ensure that Perkins would be thrown off that scent.

The diamond cutters and assayers all remarked on the clarity and beauty of the stones, the perfect cuts, top of the line color. They asked Trevor where he had acquired them, and he told them Dubai. The consensus was that if he wanted to dispose of the rest, he would probably get maximum value in South Africa, in Cape Town.

The big SUV rolled onto the superhighway toward France. Trevor had promised a late luncheon in Dijon, on the way to Paris, a four-hour trip. As they cruised along the superhighway, Trevor could not suppress the urge to incessantly look over his shoulder, checking to make certain that they weren't being tailed. The highway behind them was clear for miles.

They stopped for lunch at L'Auberge Maxime, a Michelin three-starred French country inn outside Dijon, and had a marvelous meal with wine. The tab for lunch was €1400, which Trevor happily paid in cash.

After arriving in Paris in the early evening, they checked into the Hotel de la Tremoille, in the 8th Arrondissement, a luxury hotel and spa often compared to the Ritz – with much less publicity. There would be no paparazzi lurking for a shot of Prince Harry and Meaghan, or Kim and Kanye, no onlookers.

"How do you know about such places?" Souheir asked.

"When I was in BigLaw in New York City, I got to travel on business a lot. So I hit these places on the clients' dime!" he said, laughing. "That's the only way to experience it – unless money is no object."

Which in his case now, it wasn't.

WASHINGTON, DC

Robert Perkins was livid. He was beside himself with rage over the sudden disappearance of the subject and his female companion.

The field office reported that nobody saw Trevor and Souheir leave the Dolder Grand Hotel. Nor were they on any hotel security cameras. It was as if they'd vanished.

Nor did they show up on any cameras at the railway stations and nearby airports.

Perkins had been outfoxed again by Miles, who had given his people the slip and caused Trevor and Souheir to vanish with no trace left behind.

Now it was time to up the ante, and Perkins knew exactly how to flush him out of hiding. But getting to his father, retired and living among his extended family in the Blue Mountains of Jamaica could be a very tall order – unless a relative could be identified and bribed into giving him up – which happened more frequently than people know.

PARIS

It rained all night and all day Tuesday, and the city was never more beautiful. Trevor and Souheir spent most of this time strolling on the Left Bank, relaxing in cafes, shopping and preparing for the next move.

For Trevor, Paris was where the final stage of their metamorphosis would be completed. They had slipped into Paris under their former identities; they would leave the City of Light as Eric Porterfield and Aretha Turner, citizens of the Dutch Protectorate of Aruba, one of the jewels of the Caribbean. Miles had contacts in high places there, so they were awaiting the imminent delivery of Souheir's new passport so that they could move on. Aruba, at the end of the Caribbean chain and only fifteen miles off the coast of Venezuela, was the perfect home base for them. Who would conceivably come looking for them way down there?

Robert Perkins, that's who.

The next afternoon, after a sumptuous seafood lunch at Le Dome in Montparnasse, Trevor and Souheir stopped in at the American Express office and picked up a DHL Courier package, then continued to Trevor's favorite Parisian joint, Café Tournon, just across the street from the massive gates of the Luxembourg Gardens. It was a cozy place, a friendly neighborhood bistro. Miles had turned him onto it; it was famous for its former clientele, black artists and writers in exile.

After opening the package, Trevor smiled as he withdrew the maroon passport of Aruba and viewed the photo and the name. He handed it over to

Souheir, who held it like a sacred amulet, a holy grail of sorts. It had cost him $250,000 on such short notice.

"Thank you, thank you, thank you!" she gushed, turning it over in her hands reverently, then pressing it to her chest.

"Aretha, would you care to belt out an *a capella* rendition of 'Respect' for the French diners?"

Souheir laughed heartily, her eyes dancing, her dimples even more pronounced.

He thought, *My God, she's beautiful. I'm gonna be so sorry to see her go.*

PARIS

"Final call for Air France Flight 1968 to Saint Martin, now boarding at Gate A-71," barked the public address system in Terminal A of Charles De Gaulle Airport.

It was the Thursday morning following their weekend escape from Saudi. Trevor and Souheir – now officially Aruban citizens "Eric" and "Aretha" – settled in and reclined in the comfort of first class on the nine-hour flight to the Caribbean, sipping champagne and enjoying warm hors d'oeuvres. They would change planes in Saint Martin and take the seaplane shuttle – colloquially, "The Goose" – over to Tortola. They were happy and relaxed, looking forward to the bright sun, blue skies, white sand beaches, warm clear water, gourmet food, luxury accommodations and everything else that goes with "kickin' it in the Caribbean".

Trevor had engaged a yacht broker online and made an offer to charter a used, sixty-foot sailboat in Tortola, British Virgin Islands. After they checked into the beachfront luxury villa, he would go over to inspect it personally.

As the Boeing 787 pushed back from the gate, Trevor was finally able to exhale, stretch out, fully recline his plush seat, close his eyes, and imagine spending some of his €130 million bounty. For starters, visions of a big, oceangoing motor-sailer danced in his head.

TORTOLA, BRITISH VIRGIN ISLANDS

The Brandywine Estate Restaurant, on the Sir Francis Drake coastal highway, sits high above the spectacular Caneel Bay and one of the most popular beaches on the island.

It was a short drive from the rented villa on Beef Island where Trevor and Souheir were unwinding. They had been here a week, lying on the beach drinking rum punch and smoking some of the most potent Chiba Chiba Trevor had ever inhaled. Souheir, in a stunning white bikini, showed off her gym body.

Trevor spent several hours each day down at the marina, inspecting the yachts available for charter and sale. The current plan was to charter a sixty-foot sailboat, hire a husband and wife crew, and sail the boat to St. Barts. Trevor had been on the sailing team at Amherst, but those tech dinghies imparted little but the basic mechanics. He needed someone who could instruct him in the navigation and handling of such a large vessel. He was referred to a Captain Brownie and his wife, Melda. They were an older Bahamian couple, quiet and religious, who came with excellent references, he as a seaman and crew, she as a cook and maid.

Miles and his girlfriend, Serena, would be meeting up with them in St. Barts to party and celebrate, pick up the new boat and sail off into the Caribbean. Trevor had purchased a customized Swan 98, an oceangoing motor-sailer, with retrofitted turbo engines. It was being delivered and was already en route to St.Barts. The boat had been ordered by a Russian oil trader who subsequently decided to step up to something over one-hundred feet. So Trevor was getting a break on the price.

If the crew worked out, they would offer a six-month contract to Captain Brownie and wife, while Miles and his girlfriend would accompany them on the new boat down to Aruba, stopping along the way to hit both Leeward and Windward islands. Miles told them that he was allotting six months to the Aruba leg of the trip, then he would head back to the U.S.

Miles had also offered to accompany them in house-hunting in Aruba, where they would be looking at waterfront villas north of Oranjestad, up toward the famous California Lighthouse. Trevor and Souheir planned to spend a few months acclimating to their new domicile, then set off in the new boat toward the Panama Canal and an extended trip down the west coast of South America.

They had just finished a late dinner and were driving back to Beef Island when Trevor's phone vibrated. It was Miles.

"Hey, man, where are you now?"

"We're in the British Virgins. What's up?"

"Thank the Lord you're outta Saudi, dude!"

"What do you mean?"

"You haven't heard?"

"Heard what?"

"Just turn on the television, bro!"

———《◦◦◦◦◦◦◦◦◦◦》———

So here it was. Trevor flashed on his private conversation with Prince Bindar at Ypenberg, and the revelation that something much more destructive and dangerous than Project Gemini had developed.

———《◦◦◦◦◦◦◦◦◦◦》———

"Trevor, you're a man of the world, so many things don't have to be explained to you," said Prince Bindar. "Yes, you may think that the Gemini Project is evil, but it is not inherently dangerous. Evil, yes, dangerous, no. Tell me, have you ever considered the relative natures of evil?"

Trevor, not knowing where this was going, reflected on it before cautiously answering. "I suppose so."

"What I am about to tell you may sound like a cover for Gemini, but it's not." Here he paused. "My cousin, Crown Prince Mohammed bin Salman, must be stopped. He is a murderous psychopath who would inflame the entire region, and he is only months away from obtaining tactical nuclear weapons.

His murder of Khashoggi was just the tip of the iceberg; hundreds of others have completely disappeared, and are presumed dead. Now your imbecilic president is attempting to monetize the illegal, back-channel sale of these weapons to Prince Mohammed, in exchange for a three-billion dollar cash payment parked overseas, and a multi-billion dollar line of credit to finance his real estate projects." His eyes blazed as swore, "This can never be allowed to happen."

Trevor was totally at sea. "I can't say I'm surprised," he murmured, still exiting the first stages of shock at what he'd just heard. But was the Prince telling him the truth? What if it really *was* a cover? What did he care? He had no personal stake, and nobody else would much care either. And he wouldn't be alone in this; most everybody hated the Saudis. He hated Trump as well.

"So you see, Trevor, this business is much bigger than the two of us. I know that you're aware of the ways of the world, and trust me, there is no percentage in trying to be a hero. You're certainly no fool. Things are never black-and-white; it is all lights and shadows and shades of gray. There are no 'good guys' anywhere out here. We're all part of the same hypocrisy. I myself am no saint, but my vision is different and much more positive. I intend to turn Saudi into a participatory democracy, with full empowerment of women as equals. I will modernize the country and prepare it to meet the challenges of the 21ˢᵗ century. I will immediately end the primitive and barbaric punishments and the death penalty. I will not tolerate the murder of children. And I intend to crush *Daich* once and for all, no more ISIS, no more Al Queda, no more funding and exporting jihad. Will some people be hurt by this? *Only if they get in my way.*"

Trevor heard the unmistakable warning and threat in those words.

"And let me underscore, Trevor, that this will also take down your deeply disturbed and unfit president. You will be doing the world an enormous favor."

"I understand, your highness. I despise him, too. I will keep my word. I just want to be left alone to live my life in peace. You will never hear from or about me again. But I have other concerns: my father."

It was then that Trevor offered up the contents of his briefcase, only to be rebuffed but reassured by Prince Bindar.

"Just turn on the television, bro!"

Miles's words echoed in his head as he hit the accelerator of their little dune buggy.

WASHINGTON, D.C.

Special to The Washington Post (A.P., Reuters, UPI)

SAUDI KING, CROWN PRINCE DEPOSED, NEW RULER TAKES CONTROL "FOR THE WELFARE OF THIS REGION AND THE WORLD"

New King, Backed By Saudi Air Force, Dissolves Royal Ruling Council, Detains Its Members and Declares National Emergency

WASHINGTON D.C.

Special to The Washington Post (Reuters, A.P., UPI)

King Bindar Releases Evidence of Effort by Crown Prince to Obtain Nuclear Weapons Illegally Brokered by Trump Operatives

Trump Son-in-Law Kushner Implicated in Illegal Nuclear Weapons Sale; Tapes of Secret Meetings Revealed

WASHINGTON, D.C.

Special to The Washington Post (Reuters, A.P., UPI)

Saudi Government Releases Videos of Formal Abdications, Admissions of Criminal Guilt, Ceding of Power by Former King, Crown Prince

Where is MBS? Former Crown Prince, King, Are Detained Along with Nearly 2000 Other Royals at New Facility in the Empty Quarter of Saudi Arabia

WASHINGTON, D.C.

Special to The Washington Post (Reuters, A.P., U.P.I.)

FOREIGN BANK ACCOUNTS CONTROLLED BY TRUMP SEIZED; EVIDENCE OF SECRET OFFSHORE PAYMENTS BY SAUDI REVEALED

PELOSI ANNOUNCES PREPARATION OF NEW ARTICLES OF IMPEACHMENT

WASHINGTON, D.C.

Special to The Washington Post (Reuters, A.P., UPI)

Jared Kushner Arrested, Charged with Multiple Felonies

Federal Judge Orders Kushner Held Without Bail, Citing Flight Risk

WASHINGTON, D.C.

Special to The Washington Post (Reuters, A.P., UPI)

TRUMP ATTEMPTS TO FLEE U.S., ARRESTED BY FEDERAL MARSHALS AT N.J. AIRPORT

DALLAS, TEXAS

When Robert Perkins swaggered into the private conference room atop the Petroleum Club of Dallas, he received a standing ovation from the dozen elderly men sitting around the table. The Petroleum Club remains the holiest inner sanctum of the Texas oil business, a membership-by-invitation-only private men's club, arguably the most exclusive and elite club in the world. Its membership is drawn exclusively from the 1% of the U.S. oil business. At a spry, ramrod-straight 94, Perkins was not the oldest man in the room.

After making a circuit of the big mahogany table to shake hands and greet the attendees, Perkins sat down at the head of the table and spoke.

"Gentlemen, we must all stand in awe of what we have just accomplished. Not only did we achieve the first goal of the Gemini Project, but more important, we made the world a much safer place by ridding it of *two* of the most despicable tyrants. Who could have predicted, when we met in this very room over fifteen years ago, that such a longshot effort could actually be accomplished? I remember one of you remarking at the time that the planets would have to be in perfect alignment." Here he smiled broadly. "Well, not quite, but I believe in the marrow of my bones that success was preordained by circumstances. Who could have predicted the rise of the Crown Prince and his brutality? He wasn't even on our radar at the time. But his emergence was unbelievably fortuitous, providing just the distraction we needed. Our man in-country is now the King of Saudi Arabia, the man who saved the world from a nuclear catastrophe. And, gentlemen, for the first time in modern history, a private, offshore corporation controls the largest proven oil reserves in the world. There will be no public announcements, no press releases, *nothing*. We are in an express private partnership with a sovereign nation, and until those oil reserves run dry in about thirty years, the price of crude oil will appreciate with its scarcity. It will become the world's most valuable natural resource – for which *we* will be dictating the prices and terms. We'll have more money than John D. Rockefeller ever dreamed of." He paused for effect. "And he could dream about quite a lot of it."

Everyone laughed heartily.

Perkins continued. "I'm happy to report that our parallel Project, in Venezuela, is also underway and moving rapidly toward completion. Their economy is in ruins, the country is devastated thanks to our sanctions, and now it's ripe for our regime change. When we close on that one, we will have achieved hegemony over the world's oil supply. Somewhere up there, the visionary Ronald Reagan is looking down and beaming. This was *his* vision, and he gave us the blueprint forty years ago, along with a timetable for preserving democracy as we know it."

"So this, gentlemen, is how we will completely control the political process here in America. We can *buy and own* whoever we need, and we need look no further than controlling the U.S. Senate. Remember how easy it was to buy that hillbilly bootlick from Kentucky? And the little cocksucking pansy from South Carolina and all the others? Hell, they were rushing to sell themselves to *us*! And lest anyone forget, we have other means of persuading difficult people to see things our way."

"Rob," asked one of the men, "what are the next steps?"

"Either the radical restructuring of OPEC, or its total destruction. King Bindar has already received overtures from the other members, who are scared shitless over their own futures. He is proposing a new structure, where Saudi is the center of that universe and the others mere satellites, taking their cues from us. He has guaranteed them that if they play ball, they're safe, and the responses so far have all been positive. They'd better be. When they realize how much more they can get, why not go along for the ride? After all, what is the alternative? Once we control Venezuela, we can open our pumps to maximum flow, depress worldwide prices and destroy OPEC. They'll understand that."

"Rob," asked another, "I recall that not long ago, we had a minor problem in-Kingdom. I'm assuming it was solved?"

"Yes," replied Perkins. "Our operatives tracked him to Zurich, where he temporarily gave them the slip. But King Bindar's people were also shadowing him, and he tells me that the subject was eliminated before he could leave Zurich."

Here he paused for maximum effect.

"Said they used a bone-saw," he deadpanned.

The room exploded with riotous laughter.

WASHINGTON, D.C.

It was a lazy Sunday afternoon. Robert Perkins sat in the library of his Georgetown mansion in his favorite, comfortable, leather-bound, overstuffed chair. A stack of thick Sunday newspapers was waiting on his side-table. He had given his live-in manservant the afternoon off, and his cook was arranging the tray to serve him lunch. She would prepare an early dinner before leaving at 4:00 p.m.

He was feeling exceptionally euphoric because he could count his life as a success, a triumph, the saving of America as we know it. The Gemini Project had been a total rout, a complete and stunning coup, and Venezuela was firmly under their control. Perkins liked to think that if there was an afterlife – which he doubted - his mentor, benefactor, lord and master, Allen Dulles, was surely looking down at him and smiling. For Perkins would indeed be "leaving some footprints."

Perkins sat back and reflected on his life's work and how much he had done for the posterity of America, the America he knew and loved, *his* America.

He picked up the Sunday Style Section of *The Washington Post* and began reading. Then the light in his eyes dimmed and began going out. His eyes slowly closed as his head slumped forward and rested gently on his chest.

When the cook arrived with his luncheon tray, she thought he had just fallen asleep. After unsuccessful attempts to rouse him, she stared at the broad, contented smile on his face, and realized that he was dead.

RIYADH

King Bindar bin Ahmed Al-Saud became an overnight hero in Saudi Arabia, a shining knight in a Savile Row suit, for he had deposed the brutal and despised Crown Prince, Mohammed bin Salman, whose beheadings of peaceful teenaged demonstrators was the final straw within the international community. King Bindar immediately banned all such barbaric punishments pending law revisions.

Prince Mohammed and his father, the former king, were being held in the Empty Quarter Detention Center, along with over two thousand other high-ranking royals. This was the original plan, and it was working to perfection. King Bindar was allowing the senior-most royals to buy their way out of prison, forfeiting enormous sums of cash and property, provided they departed the Kingdom and never returned. As insurance against sedition or other political agitation from afar, those so departing were compelled to identify all blood relatives remaining behind. This way, they would always be circumspect about attacking King and country.

King Bindar also commenced the expansion of rights of women, overturning Saudi custom and rules concerning guardianship. Henceforth, guardianship laws would only extend to wives and minor children. All others were free to drive and move about without restriction, and to vote for local representatives. And he declared by secret fiat to the imams at the madrassas over in the west that anyone preaching, advocating or even discussing jihad would face life imprisonment in the Empty Quarter.

The death of Perkins merely meant dealing with one of his successors, one of his cabal in Dallas.

Well and good, thought King Bindar. *This is merely the first of many steps. I have my own plans for the future.*

ST. BARTS

The blazing orange Caribbean sun was slowly dipping into the azure sea as they sat on the terrace overlooking the clear, warm water. Souheir and Miles's fiancée, Serena, were sipping their fruit drinks and discussing the upcoming trip to Aruba on the new Swan 98.

Just after they'd met up in St. Barts, Trevor took Miles aside for a private talk.

"Happy you made it down, my man!" said Trevor, beaming and enveloping Miles in a huge bearhug. "You were my go-to guy, and I couldn't have gotten outta that fucking place without you."

"Trevor, you're my man, fifty-grand and all that," said Miles. "I loved doing it. That's the stuff of life for me."

"What's left in the Caymans account?"

"It's closed. The remaining €48 million is parked in one of the Singapore accounts. Let me get the paperwork for you," he said, rising.

"No, we don't need that right now. Remember that pact we made in the back room of the Bob the Chef's, over barbecue and beer? Well, I'm making good on it, and then some. That money is all yours. Uncle Sam never needs to know about it. And *I* won't tell. Will that work for you?"

"Will it work? Will it work?" Miles asked rhetorically, gushing with delight. *"Are you serious, man? Are there KNEE-GROWS on the South Side?"*

They both laughed and ringingly slapped palms, then hugged again.

"Hey, Trevor, you know what just happened? Man, I *almost* just retired!"

"Well, why don't you?"

"And do what? Trevor, man, where would I find excitement and fun? My life would lose meaning. I live for the thrill of the chase, the adrenalin rush and high that come from a clean score. Even though this is the biggest score of my life, I can't sit down and vegetate. This is all I know. Hustlers gotta hustle, bro."

"Then you need to come on with us for about a year. After we get to Aruba, we're gonna buy a crib there, rest up, and sail for the Panama Canal. And then down the west coast of South America."

"I'm down with that," said Miles. "Is Serena invited, too?"

"Leave your main squeeze behind? Now how could we do that? This is gonna be a party boat, man!"

NOORD, ARUBA

Souheir and Serena, Miles's fiancée, sat on the terrace overlooking the water near the famed California Lighthouse, so named for the American freighter that sank offshore in 1891. The handsome, ultra-modern teak-and-glass townhouse faced west, so the sunsets were always orange and pink as the sun sank slowly into the Caribbean.

"I think the trip through the Panama Canal and down the coast is gonna be outrageous," enthused Serena.

"And we plan to do only offshore sailing with lots of stops once we get to the Pacific side. Then we'll explore the northwest coast – Colombia, Ecuador, Peru," said Souheir.

"And no open-sea adventures, thank God," said Serena. "Besides, everybody thinks the ultimate adventure is sailing around the world. Well, let me tell you, I've done some homework, and 95% of the people who set out to do it quit before they've covered a thousand miles. Know why?"

Souheir shook her head.

"Boredom. Dreadful boredom with day-after-day-after-day being the same, with the same scenery. I had some friends who tried it. They quit after they got as far as Hawaii. Couldn't take it."

Serena shifted gears and mentioned that she and Miles had decided to become engaged. Then she casually asked Souheir if she and Trevor had any particular plans.

Souheir began cautiously. "Well, I thought I would go straight back to New York, but now I'm not sure what I want to do. Things have worked out so well here for me, so…." Her voice trailed off.

"I don't mean to pry, but has Trevor included you in his long-term plans?"

"I'm not certain. We just seem to go from day to day, and we do get along so well. But long term? I don't think we've ever seriously discussed it."

"When do you think you should seriously discuss it, girlfriend? I mean, I'm not trying to be pushy, but a girl's gotta know where she stands."

Souheir sat quietly in thought.

———

"Trevor, where are we going?" asked Souheir, later that night in bed.

"Where? We're sailing to the Panama Canal, crossing over into the Pacific--"

"No, no, I don't mean that. I mean you and me. Us. What are your thoughts about that?"

"Well, I haven't really had time to think about it, everything's happened so fast. What are *your* thoughts?"

"I asked you first."

Trevor sat back and closed his eyes, as if deep in thought. "Just gimme a second," he said. Then he slowly opened his eyes. "Do you still have the zirconium ring with the tin inlay? The one I gave you in Riyadh before the escape?"

"I think so. Why?"

"Would you mind wearing it until we go down to Oranjestad tomorrow and get you the real thing?"

Her eyes widened. "Are you asking me? Really?"

"Yes, I am. Souheir, you're smart and brave and funny and gorgeous. And you're for me. I adore you. But you knew all that," he teased.

"Okay," she chirped, leaning forward kissing him lightly on the lips.

"Okay what?"

"I'm all in with you, Trevor. You saved my life. You're my hero and my love."

ORANJESTAD, ARUBA

"So we shall make stops at Venezuela and Colombia before we go through the Canal," explained Captain Brownie. "I have all the charts and instructions, and I filed a course plan with the harbormaster. We'll be doing mainly offshore sailing, putting in at different ports for the evening when we can. Any questions?"

"Is the bar fully stocked?" asked Miles, grinning. Captain Brownie took this in good humor even though he himself did not drink.

"Yes, my good sir, I have amply provisioned for the trip, and it will take even *you* some doing to drink *this* boat dry." Everybody laughed. "Now if there are no further questions, we'll cast off and get under way."

The Swan 98 slowly motored out of the marina, where Captain Brownie cut the powerful turbo engines, and automatically hoisted the mainsail and back-sail, which instantly caught the steady trade-wind. Then he unfurled the spinnaker, set all of the canvas for their heading, and they were soon rolling easily under full sail.

Miles and Serena had gone below for a nap, and all was quiet but for occasional luffing of the backsail as the headings were computer-adjusted.

Trevor and Souheir, both in swimsuits, got oiled up and stretched out alone on big, thick Turkish beach towels, lolling on the aft deck in the warm Caribbean sun, occasionally looking back at the receding shoreline.

Two hours later, they were cuddled together as the boat slipped over the horizon - and the land disappeared from view.

So did they.

AFTERWORD

THE HOUSE OF SAUD
(Summary)

KING ABDULAZIZ AL SAUD, founder of Saudi Arabia – 1932-1953 m.

Hassa Al Sudairi
(Principal Wife)
The "Sudairi Seven" Sons (Full Brothers and Allies)

Salman – King of Saudi Arabia (2015 -) - *Crown Prince Mohammed bin Salman al Saud*
Ahmed (removed from succession) - *Prince Bindar bin Ahmed al Saud*
*Fahd – King of Saudi Arabia (1982-2005)
*Sultan – Crown Prince
*Nayef – Crown Prince
*Abdul Rahman (removed from succession)
*Turki (removed from succession)
*Deceased
N.B.: In Saudi parlance, the term "bin" means "descended from;" the term "AL" means "house of". King Saud united the tribes of Arabia by taking a wife from each of the other 18 tribes. He had a total of 21 other wives, with whom he had 45 sons and countless unnamed daughters. The entire royal family currently numbers over 15,000.

Made in the USA
Middletown, DE
09 October 2021

49943935R00092